TAKE EVERYTHING

A Novel

By

Alexandra Y. Caluen

TAKE EVERYTHING

Cover design by RK Young

TAKE EVERYTHING

The playlist:

Why Should I Care – Diana Krall

Walk This Earth Alone – Lauren Christy

You'll Never Know – The Platters

Take Me Home - Cher

My Kind of Lover – Billy Squier

Maddest Kind of Love – Big Bad Voodoo Daddy

Need You Tonight – INXS

Lay All Your Love On Me - ABBA

Come to My Window – Melissa Etheridge

You Are the Best Thing – Ray Lamontagne

Well they get what they want,
and they never want it again
Go on, take everything, take everything,
I want you to

"Violet"
Music & Lyrics by Courtney M. Love
and Eric T. Erlandson

TAKE EVERYTHING

Contents

Chapter 1 1
Chapter 2 13
Chapter 3 22
Chapter 4 29
Chapter 5 39
Chapter 6 49
Chapter 7 60
Chapter 8 66
Chapter 9 80
Chapter 10 88
Chapter 11 99
Chapter 12 111
Chapter 13 126
Chapter 14 138
Chapter 15 155
Chapter 16 167
Chapter 17 177
Chapter 18 190
Chapter 19 202
Chapter 20 214
Chapter 21 228

Chapter 1

August 2016

The downstairs lounge at Chrome was packed. Richard was standing by the bar, holding a cocktail he wasn't drinking and couldn't remember ordering, when Rory, one of the stage managers and sort-of a friend, washed up beside him. "Hey Richard. Why aren't you dancing with Willem?"

Because I don't want to start crying in public. "I need to get out of here." He set the cocktail glass on the bar and turned blindly toward the stairs, almost colliding with someone he probably knew and didn't acknowledge.

"Whoa. Dude. Are you all right?" Rory stopped herself a moment before touching him. She couldn't tell if this was distress, or temper, or what.

"I have to go," he said, then remembered he'd come with Willem. There was no way he could stand riding back with him, or even getting in the car with him. The car borrowed from Willem's landlady because it was a special occasion. He dug in his pocket for his phone. His hands were shaking and he nearly dropped it.

Rory saw all this, abruptly remembered the backstage back-slapping, the 'bon voyage' and 'Anything Goes' jokes, and said, "Don't move."

Richard stopped trying to call up the Uber app. He didn't say anything in the moment before she walked away, simply stood there, now trying to breathe. Two minutes later Rory was back with her girlfriend Dana, and they were walking him toward the stairs. He didn't turn his head. Didn't try to see Willem one more time, maybe the last time. His lover was out there dancing, celebrating, not even thinking about Richard. Why should he? He didn't know how Richard felt. How could he? They hadn't ever talked about feelings. You don't do that when someone's leaving.

Neither woman asked Richard any questions. It didn't occur to him that they didn't know where he lived.

About half an hour into the after-party, Willem looked around for his date. There was no sign of him. He did manage to locate some of the other dancers in the show. People Willem only knew because of the show, like Richard. "Hey, Vicky?" He pitched his voice low, trying to be discreet. "Have you seen Richard anywhere?"

Vicky studied him for a second. "I haven't seen him." She turned to her wife. "Sharon? Did you notice if Richard went upstairs?" The mezzanine lounge at Chrome was open to the public tonight, and might have been quieter than the private after-party.

Sharon looked up at Willem too. "Oh hey. I think he left with Rory and Dana. I saw them walking out a while ago. Didn't he say anything?" Everyone at the table could see that he hadn't, and that Willem didn't know how to take it. He felt and surely looked annoyed, and upset, and worried. There was an exchange of 'oops' glances. Sharon filled in the awkward not-quite-silence, or rather the awkward gap in chatter over the house music that was pumping. "He probably sent you a text. When do you leave for the new job?"

"Tomorrow," Willem said, making an effort. He didn't know what had happened. Whatever it was, none of these people had caused it. They made room for him to pull another chair into the group, inviting him to give them the scoop on the cruise-ship contract. “It’s a hell of a gamble,” he admitted. “That’s a lot of weeks to be stuck with a situation if it turns out I hate it.” Before long they were all talking comfortably again.

Willem forgot about checking his phone until he finally left, hauling his tired body up and out to his borrowed car. *God that was fun*, he thought, glad he’d had this experience before heading off to sea. The show he’d be doing on board was nothing like this one. They’d have four days to rehearse it before their first performance, instead of three months. Everyone in the cruise cast had a list of credits as long as Willem’s. It was a Broadway revue with no story, only familiar songs with accessible dance numbers. Light entertainment. A perfectly legitimate gig, but not as satisfying as the complex original story and challenging choreography of ‘The Great Wave.’

He would have liked to spend the night with Richard. To celebrate, and to say goodbye properly. They’d only had that one night together in their short string of dates. On the thought, with the engine running but still in the parking lot, Willem got his phone and checked for a message. There wasn’t one. “Well, fuck you too,” he told the phone, letting annoyance boil to the top, swamping the hurt. He wouldn’t have thought Richard would be rude this way, dismissing him without a word. They’d clicked so fast and so thoroughly.

The lights on Hollywood Boulevard were all against him. Somehow this made him angrier. So what if they hadn’t talked about commitment. It had only been a few weeks. They hadn’t even talked about ‘when I’m back on land.’ Willem hadn’t wanted to go there, because he didn’t know if he’d like the gig. If he did, it might be years before he came back. It was good Richard did this. Better for both of them.

It wasn't until he stopped at the signal at La Brea, felt a tickle on his cheek and wiped his face, that he realized he was crying. "What's wrong with you," he said out loud. "You thought it'd be a one-night stand, and then you got six dates out of it. No harm, no foul." His inner voice, the one that constantly tried to tell him he'd done something wrong, was unconvinced.

It was late, but trying to sleep on this wasn't likely to be a success. The inner voice, always subdued by using his body, was busy telling him he'd feel better if he stopped at one of these ten thousand liquor stores. Willem turned down Fairfax and headed for a midnight meeting.

Richard was walking through the door before he realized he didn't know where he was. "Wait." Dana squeezed past him and flipped a light switch. He flinched. There was a huge orange cat sitting on a kitchen counter ten feet away. He usually liked cats. This one was squinting in the sudden light, making a face that said 'you are late.'

Rory wrapped a hand around his arm and propelled him further into the room. "Whatever is up with you, you should not be alone. Have you had anything to eat? Because I don't usually comment on how pale white people are, but you look like you're about to pass out." They were past the efficient kitchen, down a hall, and into a bigger room. She parked him on a bench, clear concern on her cute Pacific Islander face. His back was to a wall of ornate drapery. Another light switch, this time with a merciful dimmer and no more judgmental animals. Richard took stock. The bench was a continuous U-shape around a dining table. It was deep enough for a person to stretch out on, and long enough if the person was less than six feet tall. "This is your house." It wasn't quite a question. He looked up to see Dana, not Rory.

"Yes it is." She studied him, also with clear concern. Forty-something, he couldn't remember. Blonde, lovely, a successful actress. "Rory's going to feed you. Any allergies?"

"No." Richard didn't say anything else. His problems with eating had nothing to do with physiology. He didn't know how he could possibly say anything to these women. They'd all known each other for eight years, and yet they weren't friends. He couldn't call anyone at the dance studio a friend. He'd been in it, but not a part of it, all this time. Rory was as close to a friend as he did have there. They'd worked together for a while at the law firm. She was a great co-worker. And after her promotion, a great supervisor. Now he had her old job, because Dana finally said, 'this is stupid,' which everyone else had been saying for years. Stupid for someone to hang onto a boring office job when they were next-best-thing to married to a millionaire. Everyone knew Dana would never leave Rory. They were committed.

Richard sucked in a breath, almost flattened by another wave of completely-unjustified grief. *It was not love*, he told himself fiercely, grateful that Dana had left the room.

He breathed in and out steadily, focusing on the women's voices as they talked in the kitchen. It couldn't have been love. It was only a string of unusually-successful dates, with a known horizon. Willem already had the cruise contract when they met. They both knew this was a short-term thing. Richard never mentioned that six dates was the most he'd had with one person since college. Why would he mention that? It would only make him seem strange, maybe desperate. It would have made Willem wonder – or worse, *ask* - why. This was always going to be how it ended.

Rory fed him, informing him that he was staying there overnight. He did his best with the food and didn't argue. She and Dana pushed the table over as far as it would go, so he could stretch out and sleep on the cushioned bench. It wasn't cold, but they gave him a quilt. He rolled up in it with his face toward the backrest. Their big orange cat settled into the bend of his knees. When all the lights were off and he stopped hearing them move up in their sleeping loft, he finally let himself cry.

Willem didn't have much to leave. That was one of the reasons the cruise job caught his eye in the first place. His regular job at Barney Greengrass was eminently leavable. The other jobs he picked up here and there came along with some regularity, but were nothing close to stabilizing. A week or two of work on a TV show or movie, a local theater production of some kind, or a week filling in for an injured dancer in a touring show. The income, credits, and connections never really added up to stability.

His few possessions, and the clothes he wouldn't need, had gone into storage. The furnished room he'd been renting for years would be there for him again, along with the bike he had in his landlady's garage, if he didn't sign the contract extension. If he did decide to stay on board for the full year, she would rent it to someone else. That was only fair. For the few days a month that he would be on land, it would be cheaper to live in a hotel close to the harbor. Especially since he was sure he'd be able to split that cost with one or another cast-mate. That was the life of the gypsy: no privacy, no permanence, no strings. He told himself he liked it that way. That he hadn't been thinking, for the first time ever, maybe there was someone to come back to. Maybe even someone to stay for.

The Uber driver who picked him up wasn't one of the chatty types. That was fine with Willem. There was still no message from Richard in the morning. If Sharon hadn't seen him leave with Rory and Dana, Willem might have been concerned. As it was, he was angry. He let himself be angry, told himself it was good to find out the guy was this way. Much better than spending the night together and possibly saying 'can I call you when I'm back in L.A.' and maybe hearing 'no.' Maybe seeing the face that went with 'had enough.' He didn't know how well he would have handled seeing that face on Richard.

Everybody in the cast agreed with him. They had hours in between rehearsals – literally an hour in between the two or three or four-hour blocks of choreography and staging and practice – to rest. Not enough time to do anything more than eat, stretch, and gossip. It wasn't a huge cast, so by the end of day one they all knew everything about each other. Willem's cabin-mate had his own job-precipitated breakup story, which was worse than Willem's. By the end of day three he was resigned to it. The show was coming together, the cast was copacetic, and he had sixteen weeks before he had to decide if this was how he wanted to spend the last few years of his dance career.

The alternative, he knew, was to call it done. To go back to L.A. with his teaching credential, find a yoga studio, and start answering 'I'm a yoga instructor' instead of 'I'm a dancer' when people asked. He was still young, though; only thirty-four. *Almost thirty-five*, something unhelpful whispered. Young enough to still have the chops, old enough and seasoned enough that he might now be considered for more parts out of the chorus. Name parts, leading roles, not only juveniles and second leads. Maybe this gig would be enough fun that at the end of it he'd feel like going to Las Vegas, or even back to New York, to give the stage another try. The job was certainly a good credit. *Let it be*, he told himself. There was no need to think about it yet. For now, he could take advantage of the ship's facilities, enjoy having no domestic responsibilities, and have fun with his cast-mates. Get back in the groove of being part of a company. Spend eighteen weeks getting super-fit, getting a tan, and staying away from the bars.

Richard thanked Rory and Dana when they came to that pretty back room to check on him in the morning. He'd been awake for a while, going down the hall to the pretty bathroom, then looking out the windows at the pretty yard between this cottage and the big house at the front of the lot. Thinking about what 'home' meant, and why he'd never tried to make one.

Rory brought him coffee, offered breakfast, scowled at him when he attempted to decline. He gave in, accepting with half a laugh. "I don't know what your deal is," she said quietly after Dana left the room. "It's none of my business. But know if there's something you need, you can always come to me. If you want to talk or want some pot roast or just want to pet Spike."

Richard became aware that he was, actually, petting the cat with the hand that wasn't wrapped around the coffee mug. The big orange fluff monster had been up in the loft when Richard woke. "I appreciate you," he told the cat now.

Rory said, "Is there anything you want to talk about? Or *can* talk about?"

Richard bought a few seconds by swallowing some coffee. He had a person to talk to. A person he paid to talk to. He knew it wasn't the same as talking to a friend. *I need a friend*, he thought, with a sudden sharp awareness of the chasm yawning at his feet. He didn't think he could do it alone anymore. "I thought it was going to be a one-night stand," he said finally. Rory sat down, not across from him but beside him, as if she knew he couldn't stand to make eye contact. "That's kind of my specialty. Once in a while a guy will ask me out more than once. I usually say no."

"Why?"

"My therapist says it's fear of commitment."

Rory made a dubious noise, as if she didn't buy it. "You've been taking dance classes the whole time I've known you. You don't job-hop. So?"

"Personal relationships. I'm afraid of them." And he hadn't ever said that, that exact thing. "I never told him that. My therapist."

"Do you *want* a relationship?"

"I thought I didn't." Richard set the mug down hastily and covered his eyes with his hand. The other hand was buried in Spike's abundant fur. Rory didn't touch him or prompt him or in any way disturb the minute he needed to compose himself. "I'm thirty years old. I didn't think I was going to live this long. Could you please not tell anybody I said that."

His eyes were still covered. Now Rory rested a hand on his back. "Nothing you tell me this morning leaves this room."

He took a shuddering breath and it all spilled out. "I have an eating disorder. I have anorexia. I almost died in college. My doctor said if I hadn't found ballroom, I wouldn't have made it." He couldn't stop now. "I love dancing more than I love not eating. I know it's an addiction. They're both addictions. Nobody wants to put up with that. Nobody understands it. I couldn't tell him. I can't tell anybody, how could I tell *him*?"

The way he said 'him' told Rory everything. She was generally free with advice, but this was not the time. She didn't know enough about Richard or about Willem or about anorexia. He had both hands over his face now. "I think you should call in sick today," she said after a minute. "Hang out here as long as you want. I can take you over to your place later." He made a sound that seemed to signal agreement. "Does anybody else know? I mean, I'm assuming your family."

Richard couldn't stop himself from saying, "As if. If my family knew this was still a problem they would never leave me alone. I've heard enough 'what's wrong with you, just eat something' for a lifetime. As far as they know, I'm fine."

"You don't go home much, huh."

He actually laughed at that dropping his hands. One went to the coffee mug; the other returned to the cat. "No. This is a great cat."

"Yeah, he's a good one. We got him from Sam and Mateo three years ago."

"Mateo knows." Richard was surprised to hear himself say that. Maybe he shouldn't have been, after everything else he'd said. And maybe he should've taken that brief conversation for the overture it was. He could've had another friend all this time. Another one who understood dancing, and why Richard needed it. "He guessed. When he was working on 'Green

Darkness.' He told me he didn't propose to cast me for the troupe because it was all battles and he thought I was fragile. He didn't want me to get hurt. It was the right call." Another sip of coffee. He felt calmer. He'd said all this, and nothing bad had happened. "I think Dmitri knows too, or suspects. But you know what he's like."

Rory did indeed. Dmitri, the owner of Shall We Dance, rarely said anything he didn't absolutely have to say. He would and did intervene if someone was in clear and present trouble. Otherwise he let people be. That was not Rory's way. "Do you want some breakfast now?"

"Yes." He wasn't hungry – or rather, he was hungry and didn't want to eat, as usual – but he wasn't stupid. He also was deeply grateful. "Thank you."

Rory brought two plates to the back room about fifteen minutes later. She didn't say anything about what he ate, or how he ate. Simply had her own meal, gave Spike the cat a little piece of cooked egg, and kept Richard company. *Maybe I need a roommate*, he thought. He didn't want one, of course. He wanted Willem, more than he'd wanted anyone for a decade. The only good thing about the current situation, aside from the fact that he was sitting here with someone he could call a friend, was that Richard now knew he *did* want a relationship. If it couldn't be with Willem, maybe it was time to stop saying no. He was alive. Maybe it was time to embrace that.

Richard took Rory's advice and called in sick. He hardly ever did, and while he wasn't technically unwell he was also not genuinely well. They spent most of the day together, talking a lot. When she finally dropped him off he hugged her. "Thank you for this."

“I’m not going to say any time,” she said, “because I hope something that shitty never happens again. But I’ll see you at the studio.”

“Yeah. See you.” Looking around his empty, stuffy apartment later, Richard felt the floor shifting under him again. Not literally, of course. This was how a spiral could start, in the damaged part of his mind that told him he could get control of everything else by controlling food. It didn’t work. It never had. The disorder refused to be convinced by its lack of success in the past. The deeper he went into a spiral, the more out of control everything else got. He had tools to fight it now, and he would use them all. Starting with going to the kitchen to methodically compose, and then methodically consume, a meal. Careful, conscious, and if not the sort of meal that would put weight on, at least the sort of meal that kept it on.

Chapter 2

Richard had an appointment with his counselor the week after Willem left. Dr. Simon gave him a long look over his reading glasses and said, "Mr. Hollister. What's new?"

"I reached out last week. A former co-worker, someone I see at the dance studio. Told her everything."

"Everything you've told me?"

"More."

A facetious, semi-affronted glance from the therapist almost made Richard laugh. "Are you going to fill me in?"

"I'd been seeing someone. From late July through the end of August."

"Where did you meet?"

"At the dance studio, where else. You know it's the only place I go aside from work and here."

"Yeah, about that. Whatever, moving on. Define 'seeing' please."

"Everything you'd imagine." Richard had been thinking about how to tell this story. He wanted to give it the correct amount of importance. Needed to take it seriously, and present it in a way that Dr. Simon could understand. "There was one of the big summer pro shows rehearsing at Shall We Dance. It was a first full cast meeting. A lot of the dancers were people I'd met before, but some of them were new. A hip-hop guy from Las Vegas, a few martial artists from here in town."

"Martial artists?"

"The show was called 'The Great Wave' and it was about warring clans, or something, in some fantasy setting that combined Korea and Japan and China. Almost every number had some martial-arts vocabulary. Anyway, I was getting ready to leave, I was done with my thing for the day, when I heard this name. Willem van der Meer. I looked around because I went to school with a van der Meer. I was expecting someone blond." A snort from the therapist. "I found out later his family is from Indonesia. They took a Dutch name a long time ago. There's some Dutch and Portuguese in there, some Bengali, but mostly Balinese. You can imagine I thought he was beautiful." Richard had a history of choosing Asian men. "And he noticed me. That doesn't happen a lot in the studio, especially not when one of these shows is rehearsing. These men," he shook his head, conveying 'wow.'

Dr. Simon laughed under his breath. "So what did you do."

"Well, I couldn't very well hang around doing nothing for a whole three-hour rehearsal. I didn't know what to do. So I made a point of saying goodbye to one of the dancers I know pretty well, who happened to be standing near this guy, and I made a point of saying I would see him next time. I thought if the new guy was really interested, he might ask Mateo about me. And he did."

"And then what?"

"The next time I saw him, he asked me out. We had dinner, and we went to bed. It was perfect, but I didn't stay overnight and he didn't say I'll call you, and I thought that would be that. But he called me again, and I agreed to see him again."

"Which you don't often do. How many times did you see him?"

"Six. We went to bed three times. One of those times was at my place and he asked if he could stay."

"Did you let him?"

"Yes." Richard was not surprised by the 'well that's interesting' sound Dr. Simon made. "I haven't done that for a very long time. But I regretted it immediately."

"Why?" There was a distinct sense that 'the fuck' would have followed in other circumstances.

"Because he was leaving. He had a contract for an eighteen-week job on a cruise ship. Leaving the day after 'The Great Wave' closed, and by that time I knew I was in big trouble. I didn't want him to go. We never discussed whether we would get in touch again when he comes back. I don't even know for sure if he *is* coming back. It's an extendible contract."

"So he could conceivably end up out to sea for more than four months."

"It could be years. Some people really love it." There was really nothing more to say. Richard still didn't see how he could have done anything else.

Dr. Simon heaved a sigh. "I am delighted that you met someone and that it went well. I'm very sorry he's gone. You never discussed continuing?"

Richard shook his head. "From the second date on, it was just how about tonight. Never really occurred to me to ask what he thought we were doing. And all I thought was, okay, I'm seeing him again. Then I fell apart at closing night. We had dinner first, and I didn't do so well at that because I knew he was leaving the next day and I was trying to control it. You know. Got to the club and I had my supportive stage-door friend face on. Gave him a hug and a kiss, told him to break a leg, and sent him backstage. He was great, of course, he was great all the way through."

"Up to the level of the other dancers?"

Richard wanted to say yes, but this was a place to be honest. "He didn't have the big trick that nine of them did at the end. He's mostly done Broadway-style dancing. Very professional, good skills, not as deep into character as some of the others get. He held his own." After a moment he added, "I'd like to believe there's more in there. I don't think he's had a chance to do a show like that before, where there's no dialogue or lyric to tell the story. But I know that's me needing him to be phenomenal because otherwise why would I fall for him."

"There is a chance, you know, that he actually is phenomenal and that he fell for you too. It sounds as though he was awfully busy those last few weeks. He still made time for you."

"Yes. That's what I told myself all night after I walked out without saying goodbye. My friends took me home and fed me and then I talked to one of them, the one I used to work with, most of the next day. But I *did* walk out, and I'm positive he's at least mad about that. Maybe hurt. I simply couldn't face the thought of saying goodbye. One more minute with him would have made it so much worse."

The psychiatrist made a note, then said, "Well, I'm sorry. What's the takeaway?"

Richard composed himself to deliver the summary that he'd been rehearsing for days. "That in spite of everything, I'm still alive and apparently some part of me wants a relationship. So I'm going to keep working on myself, and the next time someone says hey, I know this great guy, I think you'd like him, I will let them set me up."

"And how's the disorder since then."

“Terrible. I’m using every tool. CBT, talking to Rory, getting coffee with a co-worker who always insists on getting banana bread and always insists on splitting it with me. Having lunch out with people as often as possible because it’s no easier to eat but they will notice if I don’t, so I force myself. Rory called me every night last week.”

“She’s a good friend.”

“Yes. I have to come up with a way to show her how much I appreciate it. I have an idea, but I have to wait for the right opportunity.”

“What’s the idea?”

“She was telling me how a year ago some friends accidentally adopted a dog but couldn’t have it where they lived, so Rory and Dana fostered it till the friends could move. And her cat Spike loved the dog. She still takes care of the dog a few days a week because of these friends’ terrible job hours, they’re both actors. Anyway, Spike is always happy when the dog is there, and always mopes after she goes home. So I talked to Dana and said, if I found the right dog for Spike, would you let Rory have it. They live in this tiny cottage. She said of course, do you want her to know? And I said no. This will be our secret.” He was smiling. “It’s kind of fun to have a secret that’s about something good.”

They’d been out six times. Six round trips, six weeks. Later Willem thought of that and wondered at the symmetry. He’d known Richard for six weeks before Richard, apparently, gave up. He’d been on board six weeks before he gave up.

His cabin-mate, Jesse, asked why he was never in the bar. He had the grace to ask when they were in their room. Maybe he already knew the answer. By this time

Willem thought he could trust the guy with that answer. The mere fact that he asked when they were alone said a lot for Jesse's discretion. Willem said, "The official answer is that I'd rather spend those calories at the sushi bar. The truth is I'm an alcoholic."

Jesse nodded, as if unsurprised. "I had to stay out of bars entirely my first few years. The social part was like an undertow."

"You too?" Willem was actually surprised. "How long?" He meant 'how long sober.'

Jesse knew. "Six years. The first three were rough. All of my friends were drinkers. Every one of them was like, come on, one drink won't hurt you. None of them accepted that it was never just one. I don't see any of those people anymore."

"That's the hardest part." Willem sat on his narrow bunk and stared across the room. "Giving up the booze itself was like, God, I feel so much healthier. Once the worst of the craving passed. But losing all my friends." He shook his head. "I made new friends after a while. It's not the same. I knew some of those people for twenty years."

"Yeah."

Jesse didn't ask, but Willem answered anyway. "Eight years. This is the first time I've put myself in a situation like this. Where there is literally nothing to do. I was afraid the bars would be too tempting." Then he was quiet for a minute, studying his roommate. Almost his twin: just under six feet, long-legged and slim, dark-haired and dark-eyed. And looking back at him as if to say, there is *something* we could do. "What are your feelings about fucking?"

Jesse grinned. "I like it."

"Ground rules?"

“Nobody else in the cast. And condoms.”

“That works. And no strings at the end of the contract.” Willem wasn’t sure why he said that. He still wasn’t letting himself go near a decision.

“I’m only doing the eighteen weeks,” Jesse said. “I’ve got a show in Laughlin that I have to get to.”

“Laughlin?” Willem couldn’t keep a note of dismay out of his voice.

Fortunately, Jesse wasn’t offended. “It’s an eight-month contract and a … friend of mine is working there now. Living there.”

“A friend. Will this friend mind if you’ve been banging me?”

“He’ll probably say, why didn’t you bring him with you.” Willem laughed. Then he glanced at the clock. They had time, and now that they’d said the words that went with the interested glances they’d been giving each other for weeks, it was a case of ‘why not’ and ‘why wait.’ Jesse clearly agreed, joining him on his bed. “I’m not much for kissing,” he said, setting one hand on Willem’s thigh.

“Me neither,” Willem lied, and pulled Jesse’s shirt off.

It wasn’t love, and it wasn’t forever, and that suited them both. Their personalities were dissimilar, and if their parameters weren’t clearly defined there might have been trouble. They were used to living in close quarters and could recognize the signs of imminent explosion. Those were a little more common than Willem expected; Jesse had a temper. But the ship was big enough that when someone really needed some space, the other person could disappear.

And they were busy. Their show ran twice a day except on Sundays, when the ship was on its way back into port. When they weren't getting costumed for a show, performing, or breaking themselves down, they were in the gym or at the pool or in the dining room. Everywhere they went, they were constantly reminded that this was work. If passengers came up to them at breakfast or lunch, they were expected to interact, pose, whatever. It was mostly fun, in the way that doing a character at Disneyland was fun, and without the annoying costume.

But it was still a lot like being in a cage. Willem was all too aware that without Jesse, he would have been in trouble. There were other gay men in the cast, but none of them were even nominally single, and all of them were social drinkers. He'd have been better off making friends with one of the women. And he did make friends, two of whom let him crash in their cabin one Saturday night after a near-fight with Jesse.

After that, they re-drew the parameters. Willem needed the sex – it was the only time he felt like himself, except when he was actually on stage – but he wasn't good with conflict. He tended to roll up in a ball, withdraw, avoid. They gave each other a little more space, limited the time they spent in their cabin but out of bed, and challenged each other to come up with one thing every day that was good, or fun, or that they liked about this experience. Sometimes that one thing was 'fucking you,' and they laughed about that because it was better than going into an hour-long riff on the disadvantages of the job.

Willem was dying for someone to really talk to. He wanted to talk about Richard, but he couldn't with anyone in the cast, because they'd all heard him when he was mad about it. He needed to know if he'd done something wrong or if the problem was simply him. Maybe the obvious thing to do was to text or call the man in question, but that felt pathetic and desperate. If he were going to do that, it should have been immediately. Like, hey I missed you after the show, everything okay. He could have sent that text. Maybe Richard would have written back to say yeah something came up, I'm sorry. Maybe he would have said, how do you like the cruise gig, and Willem could have told him 'I hate it, I can't wait to get back.' And maybe then he could have said, 'I can't wait to see you again.'

Willem rested his head on the wall behind him. He was in one of his hiding places, a little-traveled piece of hallway between a service complex and a block of interior cabins that were so undesirable they were usually empty. Sitting on the floor, trying not to scream. Filled with fear and disappointment, loneliness and rage. This was when he missed drinking the most. He barely missed it with a meal, or in a social setting. He missed it when he was craving oblivion. When he needed his brain to *stop*.

Eight years of successful resistance told him to stay where he was for another hour. Then it would be time to warm up with the cast, and he would be too busy to think for a few hours. Then there would be Jesse, and sleep, and he'd have made it through another day.

Chapter 3

October 2016

Richard kept going to classes at Shall We Dance. He'd been in there so consistently for so long that he could have taught the classes. That was in fact what he was shooting for. He was studying with studio head Dmitri and his associate Julia, doing a program that covered the leader's and follower's part of all nine American-style dances, all ten International-style dances, and an assortment of nightclub dances. Whether he would, in the end, teach at Shall We Dance was an open question. He hadn't yet asked if it was a possibility. For now, he went to every social event and danced with as many people as he could, leader and follower.

One of the people he danced with was Mateo. They'd known each other for four years, had performed together once, and had come close to an affair. Mateo had asked him out a few times. Casually, in a way that said he asked because he didn't want to be alone, not in a way that said he thought Richard might be his one and only.

Four years ago Richard didn't want to be anyone's one and only. He also didn't want to screw up the vibe at the studio. If he'd said yes, and they'd gone out, they probably would have ended up in bed. And then things would have been awkward, because anyone could see Mateo wasn't over someone. And sure enough, before they even did their performance Mateo had chased down Sam. Sam, who was and always would be Mateo's one and only. Taller than Willem, dark and scarred and only not-scary because he had such a gentle soul. Mateo was Richard's height, five foot eight, Filipino and almost-androgynously beautiful. Saying no to him had taken strength Richard didn't know he had.

"You were sensational in the pro show," Richard said when they finished their dance. "Both of you. When in the hell did you find time to work up that number for 'Milonga?'"

"Would you believe Sam said we could freestyle?" Mateo was smiling as they headed for the row of chairs. "But after we did it a couple of times it kind of turned into something."

"I'll say. You're not doing something this month." It wasn't quite a question. Richard was almost afraid of asking questions. He'd known all these people so long. They knew him as the guy who didn't ask, who didn't volunteer, who didn't participate except as a dancer. But that had to change, or he was never going to have a life worthy of the fact that he was, against the odds, still alive.

"I had stuff to do with Elena." Mateo had a partner for professional competition in the American Rhythm division.

"Oh yeah. I saw on the calendar you're going to the Ohio Star Ball. Things have really picked up for you this year."

"About fucking time." Mateo cut his eyes over at Richard, who was trying not to laugh. "Go ahead and laugh. You know it took a whole fucking year for them to give us a first in Rising Star."

"You should have had it by California Star Ball last year."

"Well," Mateo made a 'maybe' face. "We thought City Lights. But whatever, we got it, finally. If we get it in Ohio we'll do Open next year." They sat and watched the dancers for a while. It was only a studio social, nothing sensational was going on, but both of them watched with the teacher's eye. "Can I ask you a really personal question?"

Richard turned his head to look at Mateo. Mateo was still affecting to watch the dancers. Two years younger than Richard; intelligent, perceptive, and kind. Someone who would be Richard's friend if only he allowed it. "Sure."

Mateo didn't hesitate. "It seemed like you and Willem really connected. What the hell happened?"

It had to be *that* question. Richard took a steadying breath. "He had that cruise contract." Mateo gave him a look that said this was an unsatisfactory answer. Richard closed his eyes for a moment, breathed in again, opened his eyes. "I was falling in love with him and he was leaving. It hit me like a ton of bricks at that after-party. I ran away."

"You left with Rory and Dana."

"They took care of me. Rory is," Richard shook his head, speechless for a few seconds. "She's not even ten years older than me."

"She's everybody's mama bear. As long as you're not an actual child," Mateo qualified, because Rory's maternal moments were consistently directed only at people over the legal drinking age. Richard almost laughed. Mateo leaned ever so slightly closer, enough to bump his shoulder against Richard's, then straightened up again. "She's one of Sam's best friends. She's one of Dmitri's best friends. She's one of Andy's best friends. I never knew a lesbian who loved gay guys so much." Richard did laugh, a little. "You know Andy, right?"

"I know who he is." That was as much as Richard could legitimately say. Willem had actually been in a show with the guy once, ten years ago. But anyone who followed the Underground Cabaret knew about Andy Martin, their official photographer, formerly a Broadway dancer, now a TV star (and co-owner of Spike the cat's dog friend). "He's on 'L.A. Vice' with Victor Garcia."

"If you ever get a chance to ask him about it, I guarantee he will say 'I hate that fucking show.'" They both snickered. "Anyway, ask Rory sometime about how Andy and Victor got together. It was a fucking mess, way worse than me and Sam."

"Are you saying I shouldn't give up?"

"That's what I'm saying." Mateo slung an arm around Richard's shoulders, leaned in and kissed his forehead, then let him go. "I have to go dance with some girls."

"Yeah you do." Richard watched him go, feeling deeply comforted. He would be seeing Rory the next day; she'd said 'come and meet Spike's new dog.' A long-haired dachshund who had come to her attention by some mysterious chain of events, and who she had named (of course) Oscar. Richard would have to pretend he knew nothing of the dog's provenance. It would be a good acting challenge. If he needed to distract her, maybe he would ask her to tell the story of Andy and Victor.

Twelve weeks in, Willem knew he couldn't sign the extension. He had never imagined that cabin fever was a real, actual thing. Daily, conscious effort was required to be friendly, or at least pleasant, or at minimum civil. He was 'on' all the time: with the entertainment director and the company, with the passengers and crew, and with Jesse. There was so little time when he wasn't surrounded by people, and even then he wasn't free. There was always someone just outside the door, or around the corner.

The two point five days a week spent on land were barely better. For economy's sake, he shared a hotel room with three other cast members (not including Jesse, which was undoubtedly for the best). By week nine he'd realized that the only way to survive this was to vanish, to the extent possible, for every waking hour. The only deliberate intersection onshore was with Jesse, at an AA meeting they'd found. Both of them were handling that element of the cruise pretty well. It helped that they could be each other's support system on board.

Willem created a fake life on social media, posting photos of himself with cast-mates (including Jesse) and pretending the whole experience was one hundred percent positive. He was not going to be the guy who got a reputation as a complainer. He tried not to actively count the days, venting only to himself on Evernote. Well, and via text to Dexter Parker, a friend back in L.A.: *Dude there are days I want this fucking boat to sink*

A few hours later, the reply: *That's what you said last week. I take it you are not signing the extension*

Not not not signing. I'll be seeing you back at Barney's in January

Good, we can use a guy who knows how to place his feet

LOL anything new for you?

Actually kinda yeah. I've got a girlfriend

That was a surprise, though maybe it shouldn't've been. Dexter was tall, slim, and good-looking like Willem. He'd been making a decent living for ten years in L.A., as a professional background actor (a.k.a. extra), with Barney Greengrass as his fallback. He hadn't, to Willem's knowledge, had a serious relationship in that entire time. So that text exchange produced an actual phone call, which lasted nearly an hour. When Willem finally disconnected, he realized with something of a shock that he was actively envious. He wanted that. Even most of the footloose dancers on the cruise ship had someone they were going home to when the ship was in port. He thought he was over the worst of the Richard thing by now – it had certainly been long enough – but then he got a text from his brother giving him shit about his upcoming birthday. Like that number wasn't already hanging over his head, a neon sign blinking 'loser.'

Maybe that was why that one picture made him cringe. Inevitably, other cast members' pictures and comments showed up on his own feed. Most of them were innocuous, but then there was the one of him with Jesse at the pool. His roommate and temporary lover had his arm around Willem's shoulders and his mouth close to Willem's ear. It wasn't quite a kiss – they really didn't do that – but Jesse's expression said this was some kind of private moment. Willem wasn't looking at the camera; he was looking down, head turned a few degrees toward Jesse, smiling. If they were a real couple he would have loved that picture. Because they weren't, it made him uncomfortable. Even though he wasn't with anybody else, or even dating. There was nobody to be hurt by it, but it felt indiscreet.

And it felt like a rebuke, evidence that he was in fact a failure at something most people managed to achieve. Sure, he'd achieved things that other people didn't. But nobody cared. He knew Dexter had been through this, was still going through it: getting to the edge of middle age without a stable relationship, without a stable job of the type most people considered a career. Doing work on the fringes that most people never noticed. At least Dexter had that little apartment he'd lucked into all those years ago, in rent-controlled West Hollywood, and now he was in love. Willem had been equally lucky to find his landlady, but on the flip side that living situation was one reason he didn't have a real lover. There were so many other reasons, most of them in the category of things he didn't want to think about.

He didn't say anything about the picture, on the theory that ignoring it would keep anyone else from noticing. If he could have, he would have deleted it forever.

Chapter 4

Of course, Richard saw the photo. He wasn't stalking Willem but they'd done the Facebook friends thing sometime during week three, and neither of them had changed the status. Maybe Willem unfollowed him. He didn't unfollow Willem. He wasn't sure if it was masochism or realism: this man has a life and you are not in it; that doesn't mean your life has ended.

So Willem had somebody new. Only to be expected. Richard told himself not to take it personally.

If it hadn't been for Rory and Mateo and some of the others at the studio, people he'd known all this time who seemed to have been only waiting for him to look up and smile, those months after 'The Great Wave' might have gone differently, and very much worse. As it was, he did better than expected. The two people who knew about his anorexia didn't tell anybody else. They did make a point of inviting him along when there were groups going out to eat. Richard made a point of accepting. There was always a lot of conversation; he was never the center of attention. If anybody noticed his rituals, nothing was said. He doubted he would ever feel normal about eating, but repetition was taking the edge off his fear of being observed. It was calming the ever-twanging vibration at the back of his neck that said 'everybody thinks you're a freak.' Clearly, nobody did. Nobody at Shall We Dance, anyway, and that was his spiritual home.

He was heading into the homestretch of the teacher-training program. That kept him at the dance studio more than ever. Julia, at least, seemed to take it for granted that he would stay with the studio in some capacity. She invited him to help produce one of the ballroom-centric 'Mating Dance' shows she organized as part of the Underground Cabaret. "I could use a hand for January," she told him. "Would you be up for learning how we put these things together?"

"Of course," he said, surprised but pleased. "I've always enjoyed the Cabaret. Ever since Mateo and I did our thing. Jeez, four years ago."

"That was a good one." Julia was smiling. "The first time there was a paso doble on stage, right? And the first time two guys did a partner dance."

"Now Sam and Mateo are practically headliners." Richard regretted missing the chance (more accurately, dodging the chance) to perform with Mateo again. "Are they doing something in January?"

Julia shook her head. "No, Mateo's dancing with Elena. He and Sam are going up to the Bay Area for the holidays. Will you be in town?"

"Always. My family is best visited at odd times. Holidays are contraindicated." He watched her laugh. "Are you and the others meeting about the 2017 schedule soon?"

"Yes we are. I'll text you to let you know." That turned out to be very soon.

A day after the meeting Rory got in touch too. She texted him: *Told Julia it was a good idea getting you on the team. You know Ann & Bonnie right?*

Those names belonged to a pair of jazz dancers who'd done things with the Cabaret several times. Richard knew them from 'The Great Wave;' they'd all met at the studio, the same day he'd officially met Willem. He reminded himself that the two events were only coincidentally connected. *Yes I know them. Are you all doing something again?*

Bound to be eventually but at the moment was thinking maybe you want to come with me when I go do jazz class with them

That was as much of a surprise as Julia's suggestion that he join the 'Mating Dance' team. *You think I could keep up?*

Why not? You know 27 frickin dances already what's one more

You have a point. When and where?

"Priscilla Queen of the Desert," Rory said out of nowhere, the third time Richard went to the jazz class. Ann and Bonnie apparently had a more-or-less permanent reservation at a studio on Highland, north of Melrose. It was an easy distance from his apartment in Mid City. Rory went to dance with them there, occasionally joined by other Cabaret regulars. On this particular night, it was only the four of them, the way he'd expected the first time. When Rory uttered that complete non sequitur, Ann and Bonnie stopped what they were doing and stared at her. Richard caught up a second later. She was looking at him. "That's what you remind me of. You look a little like Hugo Weaving, you dance like Guy Pearce, and you've got this kind of seductive haughty thing going like Terence Stamp."

Richard didn't know what to say. All he could think was *what?* Ann and Bonnie, however, were both saying "Yes! Exactly! Oh my God!"

"Seductive?" he said after a moment. It was not a word he would ever have applied to himself. It was particularly disconcerting coming from Rory. 'Haughty' he could see; it was close to 'stuck up,' which he'd heard before. "How do you get that?"

Bonnie answered. "You don't often smile when you're making eye contact. It's usually after you look away. So that creates this wish to really see you smile. That's seductive. And especially because yeah, you've got the Hugo eyes, which can be more Agent Smith a lot of the time but when you smile it's like, *ungh*, Elrond." Ann and Rory both cackled.

"Nobody on Earth has ever told me that." He was half delighted and half embarrassed.

Rory suggested he should watch the movie, if he hadn't before. "But anyway, sorry about the digression. What do you think of what we're doing here."

He was relieved at the change of subject. "I like it. I appreciate you all taking the time to teach me." He was finding it easier to pick up again than he'd expected. While there had been a time, long ago, when he had some dance chops, he'd never done the kind of work these people did. He hadn't touched theatrical dance since he was twelve, and his style then was naturally very different. But as Rory pointed out, he'd been studying a lot of dances for a lot of years. Jazz had vocabulary in common with several of them, and apparently more had stayed in his body memory than he thought. "It's going to help me so much, for working with Julia." He'd have more confidence about casting the shows.

"Maybe one of these days you'll decide to do a show number again yourself." Ann drank half a bottle of water, shook her head at his doubtful look. "Never say never, Agent Smith. Aha! There it is!" She'd made him smile.

He thought about that later, after getting home and taking a good look at himself. He thought about it when he was getting dressed for work the next day, realizing that he was profoundly bored with his wardrobe. He hadn't considered what he wore for a long time. Hadn't thought about having a 'look.' He'd arrived at a formula that was mostly based on not wanting people to notice him. Maybe that was part of the whole no-expectations thing. No expectations for jobs or relationships, and no expectation of still being alive in X years. But he was. He had a good job, one that might even be called a career. He had dancing, which was genuinely fulfilling even if it wasn't something he could do full-time. He had what seemed like a lot of friends now, and those were relationships. Plus, of course, he was alive. Why not have a Look? He felt like he'd crossed some kind of border between 'unsafe' and 'safe.'

He said so to his shrink at their next session. "I'm not sure I need you anymore." It was hesitant, as if he were afraid of giving offense, which was ridiculous. This was the person who was paid to listen.

Dr. Simon didn't take offense. He said, "Great! I've been thinking that myself. You're talking to real people now. You say your condition's been easier to manage lately. Do you feel like there are still danger zones?"

"I'm sure there are. I've been hiding for a long time. I'm bound to run into situations that are going to trigger me, because there are so many situations I've avoided all these years. But I've been putting myself out there, these past few months, more than I ever have."

"And nothing bad has happened." It wasn't a question.

"Right. Everybody's got their thing. All my life I heard 'nobody's perfect' but it always sounded like someone was making an excuse for me. Like, well, you're defective but maybe you can't help it." Dr. Simon grunted dismissively. Richard didn't take it as dismissing what he'd said. His feelings were his feelings, and if his perception of other people was skewed – as it might well be – it was still where he had to start. He couldn't interrogate people about their intentions all the time. "I'm not sure I'm ready to go it alone." It felt like an admission of weakness, but he'd been in therapy for a long time. Twice a month, for years. Cutting the cord all at once felt really risky. "I was thinking once a month. I'm going to be doing some new things that may be … provocative."

Dr. Simon knew all about Richard's history. When his condition manifested, what the circumstances were, and everything since. He said, "I've always told you, you're unusually self-aware. What's the thing you're most nervous about?"

Richard gave that a moment's thought. "I'm thinking of changing my look, which means I'm thinking about being intentional about it. I've been in this same uniform for six years." Three uniforms, really. Chinos and a white button-down shirt for the office, with a blazer and tie after his promotion. Dance pants and a Latin shirt at the studio. Jeans and a twill shirt for dates or other social things. The shirt was invariably a muted blue or green, or gray. He never wore tee shirts, except when he was alone at home. Always wore an undershirt. His work and leisure shirts weren't close-fitting. Dr. Simon obviously had seen this. "I've been hiding my body for fifteen years. But it's a functional body, and I'm sick of hiding. I'm sick of dark colors." *I want people to see me.*

Dr. Simon might have heard the subtext. "And that may be triggering, you think?"

“It’ll be a big change.” *If I actually go through with it*. “Change is always scary, right?” He’d heard that so many times, right here in this office. A reminder that change scared everyone, not only him.

“Are you doing this on your own?”

“Actually I have a friend who’s a fashionista. I asked him.” Richard could tell Dr. Simon thought this was a good idea. “Sam won’t let me buy anything depressing.” The word was a surprise. He hadn’t even realized that he felt that way about his old clothes.

There was something slightly surreal about that shopping day with Sam. It was Mateo’s suggestion, when Richard confessed to discontent with his personal style, which happened to be when he was over at their place watching ‘The Adventures of Priscilla, Queen of the Desert.’ Richard never even knew what Sam’s day job was, before that. Then he’d gotten a look at the way Sam dressed for work, and the way he and Mateo both dressed for special occasions. Combinations he wouldn’t have thought of, flattering and distinctive. Personal. He wanted a look like that.

They didn’t go to the tux shop Sam managed. The day began at Richard’s place, where Sam went through his closet to get an idea of what would be staying. “Are you attached to these jackets?” he said doubtfully.

Richard looked at the three blazers in question: one battleship gray, one navy, one black. “I hate them all,” he said. It was a revelation. “I went to the Men’s Wearhouse two years ago and said I wear khakis or black chinos to work, what goes on top. I don’t think they even fit right.”

Sam had him put one on, looked at the results, and raised his eyebrows. “That one doesn’t.”

"'Help me, Obi-wan Kenobi, you're my only hope.'" It was the closest thing to a joke that Richard had ever said to Sam. He got a beautiful smile for it. "Let's go spend some money."

One result of being out with someone who was five inches taller and weighed close to fifty pounds more was a non-negotiable lunch. As far as Richard knew, Sam wasn't aware of his eating disorder. Like Rory a few months before, he didn't say anything about what or how Richard ate. Instead, after cleaning his plate, he sat back and said, "Mateo thinks you're sexy."

Richard swallowed, put down his fork, and looked up. He wasn't sure if he should be alarmed. Fortunately, Sam was smiling. "You don't mind?"

"You know how he is. If he likes something, he says so. Or vice versa." Sam studied him for a moment. "How's your workplace? Any homophobes on your team?"

"I haven't had any issues. But then my whole, what would you call it, presentation? Kind of non-obvious."

"What would be obvious?"

That was a good question. He couldn't really see stepping away from the chinos and button-down at the office. The blazer was for going in, going home, and meetings. What should his clothes be telling people at meetings? Maybe that he wasn't as boring as Records Manager sounded. How much of himself, his personality, did he want to show? Did he, in fact, want to be noticed? And if so, what was the right way to get noticed? "I guess pink velvet would be obvious." Sam laughed. "Too obvious for work, anyway. I don't even know what's out there."

"Would you wear pink velvet on a date?"

"Jeez, I never thought about it. Why did I even say pink velvet? Is that a Freudian slip?" They were both laughing now. Sam made a 'maybe so' face. "Let's do work first. Along the way if I trip over something I like, you could tell me if I'm way off."

"All right. First let's get you some boots."

Richard was tempted to question that, but only until he tried on the cowboy-styled ankle boots. They gave him almost two extra inches of height and made his legs look a mile long. "Why didn't I ever think of this before?"

Sam must have realized this was a rhetorical question. He simply suggested getting more than one pair. Richard opted to secure the first pair – black and white fake snake – and then come back after he knew what else he'd be wearing.

Being there with Sam made the process so much easier. Every time Richard was inclined to retreat to the familiar (safe) non-colors, Sam gently steered him away. He also didn't let Richard spend too long on any one problem. After determining that the office did casual Fridays, he decreed that Richard needed only two blazers. Those turned out to be soft-textured lightweight tweeds, one in a mix of gold and green, and the other a blend of blue and purple. Then Sam found a shawl-collared cardigan, natural cotton with denim-blue accents. "That's for Friday," he said. "The black and white boots go with the heather jacket and your black chinos. Let's get those brown crocodile boots to go with the green and your khakis." He had Richard take pictures of what they had so far, for reference, so they could take things down to the car before going on to the next phase. After that, there was a break for a beverage and some chat about what Sam and Mateo were doing next. But the older man made it clear this day was all about Richard. Discovering what he liked, what made him comfortable while at the same time making him feel good about himself. There were four new silk ties, because Sam said the knit ones he had were only good for tying somebody up. Of course that gave Richard a fairly tantalizing mental picture, which may have been Sam's intention.

It was exciting and fun, but exhausting. By the time he was completely squared away for work, Richard wasn't sure he even wanted to bother with leisure wear. Sam made him eat some more, asking for one more hour. They'd been in almost every store at the Century City mall that carried menswear. In that last hour they returned to two, leaving with two pairs of Vans loafers and eight shirts that Richard would never in a million years have picked out for himself. One of them was some sort of thin velvet, bright rose-pink with a multicolored paisley design. It should have been revolting. He was pretty sure his parents would hate it. But it brought out all three colors in his eyes, and it made him smile.

After he took Sam home, with first a handshake and then a hug to go with the 'thank you,' Richard went back to his place and unloaded his new image. He unpacked, de-tagged, and hung everything up. Then he packed all the things he never wanted to wear again into the shopping bags, dumped them by the front door, stripped, and lay naked on the bed. He felt like he'd shed his skin, or like a butterfly that had just crawled out of its chrysalis. Tender and unready, but fresh. Rejuvenated. Terrified.

Chapter 5

Toward the end of the contract, Willem was hanging on by a thread. The feeling of confinement was awful. The fact that the rest of the cast felt the same way was only marginally helpful. His lack of foresight about the Jesse situation was, in retrospect, typical. It wasn't intrinsically a bad thing, but they'd become overly dependent on each other, and the things Willem wasn't able to talk about had begun to eat away at his equilibrium. He wanted to stand up at the meeting and say 'I'm an alcoholic, and I'm desperate for love, and I am using somebody, and I hate myself even though he's using me too.' He couldn't, because Jesse was there. And if he found a different meeting at this late stage, it would be all too obvious why.

The last four weeks on board ship were the hardest. From the week before Christmas to the week after New Year's, there were extra shows to do and the audiences weren't there for that. People were drunker than usual, louder than usual, and more apt to harass the cast. The girls came in for the worst of it, but the men caught their share. "I swear if somebody grabs my ass again I'm going to break his or her fucking hand off at the fucking wrist," Jesse said when they were finally behind their closed door, at two in the morning, with only a few days to go.

"Thanks for the warning." Willem was too tired to want to screw anyway, but saying something light or flirty had defused Jesse's temper more than once. It was worth a try.

And it worked this time, too; he laughed. "God. I wasn't sure we'd make it for a minute there. Everybody is sick of this. I don't think anybody extended."

“I hate every one of these songs, every one of these dances, and pretty much everybody on this boat,” Willem agreed. He flopped down on his back, too tired to wash up, glad he’d gone to the men’s room on their way out of the performance lounge. He got his shoes, socks, and pants off without sitting up, then wriggled out of his shirt and briefs. He wiped himself down with the shirt and dropped it on the floor with the rest. “Ugh, I’m disgusting.”

“No you’re not.” Jesse was sitting on the edge of his bed, looking across the room. “You were a lifesaver this trip.”

“You too. Still going to Laughlin?”

“Oh yeah. Eight shows a week but they get re-worked once a month. It won’t be like this. Same damn thing over and over and over again.” Jesse stripped, much as Willem had, then went to their tiny bathroom. When he came out Willem was half-asleep. Jesse leaned over to press the side of his face against Willem’s for a moment. Not a kiss, but something like it. “Thanks.”

“You too.”

Willem thought about that a lot after his return to Los Angeles. He moved in again with his landlady, retrieved his stuff from storage, went to talk to the manager at Barney Greengrass and got back on the schedule. He knew it was going to be short-term, though. That cruise gig had accomplished one thing: he’d finally admitted to himself that he didn’t want to be alone anymore. He wanted someone to talk to, someone to come home to. The almost-a-relationship with Jesse had kept them both out of the bars, maybe kept them from going completely stir-crazy. And it hurt, a little, that Jesse had moved on to someone, someone who was waiting for him. Someone he would kiss. Willem knew he would, knew he'd lied about it the way Willem had, because he had come so close to it so many times. As if it were the natural thing to do, but not with Willem. That was for someone else. Someone who mattered.

Willem wanted a kiss so badly he almost took the first offer he got, which was basically his first day back on the floor as a server. But that offer was from someone he didn't even know, much less like, and he was tired of pretending he was okay with shit like that. He went home that night, put together a resumé, and sent it to every yoga studio in West L.A.

Dexter was at the restaurant the next time Willem had a shift. The work being what it was, they didn't have time to catch up until after closing. They went across the street to the bar at Ocean Prime, annoyed the hell out of the bartender by ordering coffee, made up for it by ordering food, and talked for three hours. From Willem's point of view, Dexter's most interesting news was about the tap-dance piece he'd performed in December, and the new jazz piece he was working on. "I'm going to submit it to the Underground Cabaret," he said, looking nervous. "My girl and I went to see their December show, and I was like *damn*. Feeling like a fool because all these years they've been doing it, I've never seen them. I didn't even see that thing you did last summer."

"Yeah, I know," Willem said dryly. "I'll lend you my copy of the DVD. You're not going to believe the closing number."

"So I didn't hear from you much the last six weeks or so. Nothing new to say?"

Willem shook his head. "I was keeping it together but just barely. Thank God it was only eighteen weeks. Every one of us was fucking psychotic by week fourteen." Dexter tried to stifle a laugh. "So your girl is still your girl, huh?"

"I am *crazy* about her." Dexter had a soft smile on his face. "She is so smart, and so fine. She gave me so much good advice."

"About the acting thing?"

"Rita's worked in casting for a while now. She's about ready to start pitching herself as a casting director for indies. She told me all my stuff looked too nice. So I got some new photos done, and put up a new video. I'm looking for a new agent."

"I saw that video. The Glengarry one, right? It was good. Your old agent hasn't done you many favors."

"Yeah, that's what she said." It wasn't strictly true. Dexter averaged over a hundred days a year of paid film work. But if he was ever going to break out it needed to be soon; he was thirty-six.

Not much older than Willem. The thought made him say, "I'm about to throw in the towel. I'm tired of leaving people. I'm tired of being a chorus boy, being Guy at Table Five, maybe getting a commercial two or three times a year. I sent out my resumé last night. The yoga one." It included a short list of notable credits, because there was literally no business in Los Angeles that didn't like to puff up any entertainment-industry connections it could. "Before this trip I was thinking I might go to Las Vegas, or even back to New York. Then halfway through I was like, why. What do I need to prove. I've done every major American musical. I've danced in a show with Andy fucking Martin, goddammit." Dexter laughed. Willem smiled into his coffee. "Pretty sure he wouldn't recognize me, but whatever."

"You never know. You're a good-looking guy."

“Back at ya.” They clinked coffee cups.

Willem wasn’t sure what to expect from the yoga job search. He’d never done it before, and the stories he’d heard while he was doing his certification made him think it could take a while. But maybe a lot of people had left the field (or left town) recently. Within a week he spoke with managers at eight different studios. Swiftly following those conversations were five formal interviews, followed by invitations to give teaching demonstrations at three places. At the end of two weeks he had two offers. One was from a large chain studio in Santa Monica, which wasn’t exactly convenient. It was a full-time job, which was good; but at an hourly rate below what he averaged (with tips) at the restaurant. Only the benefits made it attractive.

The other offer was from an indie shop called Tidal Flow Yoga. It was near the Beverly Center, much closer to where he lived. The manager proposed that Willem would teach three group classes daily that had a set progression. He’d have the option of designing a fourth class after a ninety-day review. And he’d be able to do private lessons or coaching, as many hours a week as he wanted, paying the studio a floor fee. When he asked about the setup he was told it was inspired by a nearby dance studio called Set The Barre. “They can’t afford full-time instructors, wages and benefits and all that,” said the manager. “Neither can we. So we pay a high hourly rate for part-time, and our students have access to high-quality instructors on a much more flexible basis.”

Willem asked for a day to think it over, but he was pretty sure he’d take that offer. While he was building up a yoga clientele, he could keep working at the restaurant. He could take enough industry work to keep his name in front of union productions. Keep his insurance through the Screen Actors Guild. He'd have greater income stability, and a path toward an honorable career off the stage or screen. In time he'd be able to do only the one thing. Have only the one job, and maybe do well enough with it that he could get his own place. He hadn't ever lived in an apartment by himself. That seemed like a baseline requirement if he were seriously going to look for a life partner.

Inviting someone back to a rented room was one thing when you were two years out of college and flat broke. He'd taken Richard back to that room twice, or rather Richard took him. Willem hadn't thought anything of it until after the fact. The night they'd spent together was at the other man's apartment. Richard, with his office job and his snake hips and his guarded hazel eyes. Richard, who'd kissed him like he mattered and then walked away without saying goodbye. Willem was astonished to realize that the hurt was still fresh.

He suddenly wondered if it was because Richard had that stability. The job with benefits, the apartment, the car. He was settled, in a way Willem clearly was not. That feeling of connection might have been all on Willem's side. Richard might have thought it was simply a fling. A guaranteed short-term, no-strings fling. The encouraging words in that light, always-hoarse voice, the smile and the hug and the kiss before Willem went backstage, all might have been no more than he'd have given any casual lover.

But it wasn't casual, Willem insisted to himself. He would have sworn it wasn't. He would have sworn, from Richard's hesitancy – almost reluctance – when Willem asked to spend the night, that this was something he very rarely (if ever) did. The morning after, it seemed they both agreed that waking up together was a fine thing. Maybe, after the fact, the contrast was too great. Maybe the little bit of glamorous shine that came with 'I'm in a show, I'm in SAG' looked tarnished in the light of day.

It was the first time he'd had these thoughts. He felt no shame or embarrassment – his minimalist lifestyle had kept him solvent when others would have gone into debt – only acceptance. If he wanted a real, settled life he needed to change.

He wondered if Richard would notice. Wondered if he still followed the Facebook feed. In case he did, Willem made a point of posting about it when he accepted the job at Tidal Flow. He'd been so tempted to comment on Richard's post about the 'Mating Dance: Island Time' production he'd worked on.

Then, the next day, he forgot all about Richard. He was at work, at the restaurant, when the whispers started: someone had been killed. An accident, here in L.A. The customers were all talking about it, but he had to go online to get the facts. And then he went to find Dexter, also on shift that day, because they both knew the man who died. "This is *horrible*," he said. "It's Ray Daniels." A rising star on the cop show 'Ten-31.' Only thirty-four years old. He'd danced in 'The Great Wave' with Willem, and worked as a dance extra several times, in the past, with both Willem and Dexter.

There was nothing to be done, and really nothing to say. They hugged for a minute, then went back to work.

Richard got the text around noon and almost didn't look at it. Anything from Julia was going to be something he could deal with later. But he had a minute, so he opened it up. It was a group text from

Julia's daughter Grace. He read it twice, then went to his workstation to check the news, feeling sick. Ray – handsome, happy Ray, married to Julia for little more than a month – was dead. Killed right outside Shall We Dance when a phone-distracted SUV driver jumped the curb. The message said 'no calls please.'

Richard felt helpless. The studio staff, and all of the regulars, would be devastated. A photo online showed the front of the studio, heavily damaged. They would surely be closed for a few days. Nobody owed him any updates; probably no one would think of contacting him. Grace must have simply sent the text to everyone in Julia's contacts list. There must have been so many people on that list who she knew from the dance studio. If he hadn't been growing closer to some of those people over the past few months, he might not have even realized how intertwined all their lives were.

Then he got a second group text, this one from Mike Borodin, his occasional jazz classmate. Mike and his wife Paula had been walking out with Ray and Julia when the accident happened. They were uninjured, thank goodness. He sent a reply: *So glad you and Paula weren't hurt, so sorry that happened. Please let me know if and when there is anything I can do*. He didn't expect a reply, not even the brief acknowledgement he received. He'd never been on the outside of a situation like this before. He had been the one in the hospital. The one people expected to lose.

He wasn't good for much the rest of that day, going about his work mechanically, even less talkative than usual. When one of the records clerks finally asked what was up, he said, "A friend of mine was killed in an accident." She looked shocked, patted him awkwardly, and quickly spread the word. Richard wondered if it was a stretch to call Ray a friend. But they'd all been acquainted for so long. There were coffees and dinners and nights out at Chrome, for the Cabaret performances. Jokes and dances, handshakes and hugs. "Oh shit," he said out loud, and picked up his phone again. Ray had really bonded with Mike, but also with Mateo and Sam. He sent a text to Mateo: *Such horrible news, can I help?*

A reply came immediately: *I don't know but can you come over tonight? Like ASAP?*

Of course. Be there right after work. I'm so sorry honey. He sent the text without even questioning the endearment.

As usual, Richard didn't feel like eating. He had no idea what state Sam and Mateo would be in, assumed that food wasn't going to be the first thing on their minds, and debated using this as an excuse not to eat. *Don't be an idiot*, he told himself. Falling off the wagon for even one night had proven to be a slippery slope in the past. The longer he went without eating, the less he wanted to eat, and the more ornate the ritual required to force himself to eat. So instead of going directly to West Hollywood, he went from the office to the mall for a poke bowl. And instead of doing what his disorder demanded –having all veggies with the fish, instead of rice – he got half rice. The starch would help keep his brain level, whatever happened that night.

Of course, getting the rice meant a certain amount of ritual. A poke bowl was nearly impossible to divide into equal portions, so he had to outsmart the disorder. It all took some time. But he knew Sam and Mateo wouldn't blame him. They probably wouldn't even notice; ASAP meant 'as soon as possible,' after all, not 'immediately.'

Parking in WeHo being what it was, Richard pulled into the small lot behind Shall We Dance. He recognized Mike's Jeep there. If Dmitri came in, he would recognize Richard's car too. The studio boss wouldn't call for a tow truck. Richard didn't go around to the front. Instead he walked down the alley before turning onto the boulevard toward Sam and Mateo's place.

Chapter 6

Mateo opened the door, looking tired. "Hi sweetie, come on in. Have you had something to eat? I've got stuff but it's not exactly assembled." He closed the door behind Richard.

"I'm fine, I got something at the mall. Where's Sam?"

"He'll be out in a minute. He's on the phone with Vince." Another studio regular, another friend of Ray. "This sucks so fucking much." Mateo flung himself onto the couch. His black cat was instantly there. "Hi Frida. Pachuco is sticking with Sam," he told Richard, referring to their other cat. "He went to work today trying to tell himself it was going to be okay."

"Were you at the studio when it happened?"

"No, Elena and I were over at Matsumoto's getting some costume shit taken care of. Dmitri called and said don't come back here. He is fucking *wrecked*." Mateo's eyes were wet, obviously not for the first time. "We were all hoping. Then this morning, nothing, and it got later and later and we were like, if there was good news we would have heard by now. Goddammit." He wiped his eyes. "My sister was over there too, she works there, and we brought her back here. She actually cooked dinner for us. I think it's the first time she's ever done that." Richard didn't say anything, only let him talk. Mateo was not the strong silent type. He was the strong Say Everything type. He said, "She stayed all night. We were almost to the point of going down the street to score some weed and she was like, get a grip, guys. She made us play Scrabble and drink wine. We never exactly chilled out but we kind of passed out. She was gone when Sam woke up but she'd been down to the supermarket and there was all this shit from the bakery." Half a laugh, and more tears. "I've been on a sugar rollercoaster all day. When did you hear?"

"Grace's text."

"I can't even imagine what kind of state Julia is in." Sam came out to join them, carrying the big Ragdoll cat. Mateo gazed at him worriedly. "Hey honey. How's Vince?"

"He's hanging in there. Hi Richard. Thanks for coming over."

"I don't know why I'm here," he said honestly. "I want to help but I don't know how."

"Where did you park?"

Sam's question seemed like a total non sequitur, but he answered. "Behind Shall We Dance."

"Could you stay?" Mateo that time. Richard turned his head, questioning. "Could we totally, absolutely abuse your friendship and take you to bed?" God only knew what his expression said; Mateo actually laughed a little. "Not to fuck. I need an extra pair of arms. Could we make a Sam sandwich?"

Sam was still standing, leaning against the wall beside a framed photograph of him with Mateo. His face was buried in Pachuco's fur. Richard gazed at him for a moment, then turned back to Mateo. "Whatever you need. If you need to fuck we can do that too." Mateo's expression now was noncommittal, as if he wasn't sure that was a good idea but also wasn't sure he didn't want to do it anyway.

Richard hadn't been with anyone since Willem. All the dates he'd been on since then had been conducted entirely in public. He didn't actively *want* to have sex with either of these men, but all those years of therapy told him that uncharacteristic sexual behavior was a common reaction to bereavement. And he couldn't imagine it would be in any way unpleasant. They were both fit, attractive, sexy men. Both his friends. He realized he was talking himself into it, which in other circumstances would have been funny. Maybe a change of subject was called for. "What do you have to drink around here?"

An hour later, they were all on the couch and well into the second bottle of some smooth, dark red wine Mateo said was from Gold Country. Sam was angled into the corner with Mateo on his lap, leaning against his chest. Sam's feet were on the coffee table; Mateo had one foot there and one on the couch. Richard was stretched out with his head on Mateo's thigh. Both cats were wedged in alongside his legs. They'd been talking about Ray, of course. Now Mateo somewhat drunkenly dropped a hand into Richard's hair and said, "Tell us a story."

"What kind of story."

"Your story." Richard tipped his head back to make eye contact. Mateo and Sam were both gazing at him. "Has your voice always been like this?"

"Like what?" Richard knew perfectly well what he meant, as Mateo could certainly tell even through the two hefty glasses of fifteen percent alcohol. "No. One time I was in the hospital and had to be intubated. My vocal cords were damaged."

"One time?" That was Sam.

Richard swallowed some more wine, then stretched his arm out to set the empty glass on the coffee table. "I was in the hospital three times. The first time I was fifteen. It was an overdose. My mother told the doctors it was an accident. Maybe it was." He still wasn't sure he'd genuinely been trying to kill himself. All those years of therapy (and the fact that he hadn't tried again) had halfway convinced him it was the classic cry for help. "Had my stomach pumped that time. Three months out of school, and no more auditions. I was a child actor." That wine had really pushed some doors open. Mateo was petting his hair. Sam's free hand rested on his chest. It felt like the safest place he'd ever been, or could ever possibly be. "I was small. Till I was thirteen I could pass for eight or nine. My mother was ambitious. When I got a little taller and put on some weight she didn't handle it well." He was sure both men heard the subtext: so neither did I.

Mateo made a sound that was something like a growl. Sam patted Richard's chest and said, "Sometimes I feel lucky I was in foster care."

Richard almost laughed. "She meant well, I think. Anyway, the second time I was in the hospital it was for a bad case of food poisoning. I was eighteen. I was full-blown anorexic by then and lost my senses of smell and taste. Couldn't tell something went bad."

"Jesus," Mateo said. "You got those back, though, right?" His tone said a lot about his love of food.

It made Richard smile. "Yeah, pretty much. As long as I stay hydrated and I'm conscious about what I'm doing." Without quite realizing it, he laid his hand over Sam's. "The last time was the worst. That was when I was intubated. I was technically dead for a minute." Mateo's hand slid down to the side of his face. "I was almost twenty. I wasn't trying to die." He was sure about that. "But you couldn't call it an accident. My heart's been damaged. I'll never be strong. I never was." None of them spoke for a minute. "When I got that text I had a moment of wishing it could have been me. Not because I want to die, but because Ray shouldn't have."

"I hope that driver rots in hell," Mateo said, very precisely. "I hope she never sleeps through the night again. I hope she goes to fucking *jail*. Let's finish this bottle." They all shifted, separating and levering up. Mateo put together a snack and Sam fed the cats. They talked about the trip to the Sierra when they bought that wine. Richard listened, grateful that everything he'd said had been so matter-of-factly accepted. He ate what was offered, in his typically odd way. As usual, his hosts didn't mention it.

When they suggested he stay, he said, "Of course," even though the intervening hours had settled everyone down. They took turns washing up. Mateo provided a fresh toothbrush for Richard, and some pajama pants. Then without any discussion they all got in bed. Mateo turned into Sam's arms. Richard pressed up against Sam's back. He was thinking how nice it was to have a body next to his when he fell asleep.

It was nice, but it was strange having someone there, someone he wasn't used to, and especially two someones. Richard slept fitfully and woke early, slightly disoriented. A quiet trip to the bathroom, then getting dressed. He could tell by the way Sam and Mateo were wrapped around each other that they would make love when they woke up. Before he left the room he glanced over and saw Sam watching him, faintly smiling. Richard smiled too. Sam made a move that said 'come here' so Richard went over and leaned down. Sam said, "Thanks for staying," wrapped a hand around the back of his neck, and kissed him. Soft, light, mouth closed. Simply affectionate.

When he let go and Richard drew back a little he saw that Mateo was awake too, sleepy-eyed and clearly aroused. Another light kiss, another smile. "I'll see you soon."

Mateo said, "Don't forget breakfast," and put his mouth on Sam's throat. Richard left the room, let himself out, walked down the almost-quiet boulevard and up the alley. A coffee shop a couple doors down from Shall We Dance was already open. He went in and ordered a breakfast sandwich and a large latte, sitting down to take his time eating. As usual, he felt like the whole world was watching, even though there was no one there but the barista and she clearly had other things to do, like lean on the counter looking hungover. *Me too*, Richard thought, amused. He wouldn't have missed that night, though. Not for any morning-after headache. Even though nothing physical had occurred, he knew they'd passed some kind of friendship milestone.

He was slightly late to work, owing to having to get home, shower and dress, and then battle rush-hour traffic to Century City. He told the office administrator why and she said "Why did you even come in?"

He had to think about it. "Well, I guess because life goes on. He was my friend but there's nothing I can do for him. There's nothing I can do for his wife. I spent the night with some friends who were closer to him than I was. They're better this morning. So I guess I've done what I can."

"Sometimes that's all we can do," she said with a consoling pat on his arm. "Let's get coffee later."

The night they all heard about Ray, Willem was not at all happy about being alone. A year ago he would have been on the phone, trying to find one of his occasional hookups who was free and amenable. Now that felt like taking the easy way out. He thought Ray deserved better than that. If Willem couldn't be with someone he loved – because he knew how much Ray loved Julia, he'd heard all about it during 'The Great Wave' – then he should be alone. Show some respect. Deal with it like a grown-up. So he went to a meeting, where nearly everybody shared a distracted-driving story. The thought of his own life being cut off that way wouldn't stop cycling. What would he have to show for it? What would anyone remember? Would anyone even miss him?

And what kind of self-pitying bullshit was that. An English friend once said something was enough to make a cat laugh. Willem thought that applied pretty well to his train of thought. He had a few things to show for his life, a few good performances, which could be seen forever thanks to the internet. His brother and sister loved him. His parents still loved him, even if they were showing a little fatigue with his gypsy life.

Well, so was he. They would be happy when they got his card – an actual card, sent through the actual mail, because they were old-fashioned – with the news about the yoga job. The short letter saying, I've decided it's time to have a real life. Not quite the same 'real life' as his siblings, obviously. He wouldn't be marrying an opposite-gendered person and settling down close to home, close to Urbana, to raise a new generation of ever-more-diluted post-colonial Indonesians.

He would stay in Los Angeles, because this was where his friends were. Where his life was. And where, he hoped, he would find real love, the kind of love that Ray and Julia had. He didn't have anyone specific in mind. He would have sworn he didn't. So he didn't know why he found himself online at two in the morning, looking at Richard's Facebook feed. There was nothing new. Nothing since the post about 'Island Time.' The photo of Richard with Julia and Ray, and that Filipino hottie from 'The Great Wave' with his ballroom partner, the Salma Hayek lookalike. Richard smiling in that way he had, not looking directly at anyone. Almost as though he was afraid to be caught being happy.

Willem looked at the people who'd engaged with the post, slowly realizing they were all locals. The one thing he knew about Richard was that he grew up in New York. Did he have a family? He must. There had to be someone. Willem didn't even know how old he was. He'd assumed Richard was his age, but he might be anything up to forty-five. His jawline was firm and his hands didn't have the ropey veins of age. But there were fine lines on his face and a trace of gray in his hair, an autumnal blend of many shades of brown.

That thought made Willem remember the threads of silver beginning to show in his own hair. It was a good look for him, now that he wasn't going to try to look twenty anymore. It served his new purpose to look a little older, more mature. To look like someone who could be trusted to give good coaching, good advice, good adjustments.

Would he look serious enough for Richard now? *Why am I thinking these things.* Because, he realized, that was what he wanted: to go back, to start over, to make it real. How long would be long enough?

He knew where to find Richard. The question was when. Maybe he would know once he was settled into the new routine. Once he had become his new self. Surely it wouldn't take that long. He was used to becoming someone new. Besides, this was the first time he was really doing it for himself.

He found himself talking about it the next time he went to a meeting. As usual, he tried to make it funny. "Is thirty-five too young for a midlife crisis?" The group mostly laughed. Willem shook his head. "I'm going through some career changes and I've started thinking about why I chose my major in college."

Someone asked, "What did you major in?"

"Kinesiology. All you hear is how health and fitness are growth industries and the world will never stop needing fitness professionals, right? Seemed like a thing I could do without locking myself in an office."

"Ugh, tell me about it," someone else said. "One of the reasons I started drinking was to relax after eight hours of nitpicking emails."

Another person said, "Same, kind of. Grad school and nitpicking teaching assistants."

Willem smiled and listened, not minding that other people were steering the discussion. He'd said enough to show up, and he was never going to talk about the seed that had grown into his addiction.

Over the next few weeks, Willem saw Dexter from time to time at the restaurant, but things were happening for his friend. Their shifts overlapped less and less frequently. He promised to try to see the Underground Cabaret's February show, since Dexter was performing, but missed it. Or rather, opted out in favor of a well-paid three-night shoot for a nightclub scene in a movie. He promised Dexter he'd see the piece on video, and he meant to, but he was so busy. Teaching yoga was more tiring than working on a show. When he got to his room, all he wanted to do was sleep. *To sleep, perchance to dream*, he thought woozily one night. He couldn't remember where the line came from.

A day or so after that performance something really big happened. Willem got a call from Dexter, which he missed because he was in the middle of a class. He hoped they'd connect when he called back; he wouldn't have another chance to talk for hours. Dexter answered in a way that said this was business. "Thanks for calling back. I have an offer, and it's a good offer. Rita helped set it up. I just need you to tell me if it's in horrible taste."

"Well, is it porn?"

Dexter laughed. "No. Thanks for that. It's a guest role on 'Ten-31.' Playing a crime boss. They came up with this storyline to cover losing Ray, where his character was killed because he looked like this criminal. Rita knows his agent and she threw me in the ring because at a glance I look so much like him."

"Wow, she really is smart. No, it's not in bad taste." Willem didn't even have to think about it. "It's actually a way to keep him in front of the audience all season. Does it go through to the end?"

"Yeah, it does. It'll remind people he was a good guy. Dana Richardson – did you ever work with her? She plays the captain? – anyway, she said she knew they had some unused footage that they could cut in. They can do some flashbacks for her and the gal who plays his partner. I don't even know what they were thinking of doing about it before she put this idea on the table."

"It was her idea?"

"Yeah, I think so. She and her girlfriend knew him. Personal friends. She was like, damn it, we can't pretend he never existed."

"You should take it. That's great, Dexter. Good for you. Oh shit."

“What?”

“Next class, I have to go. I’ll start watching, I promise. You’re going to be terrific.” They got off the line, and Willem went to have a snack before he had to teach again. Carefully and consciously telling himself that wasn’t what he wanted, he didn’t miss it, and he wasn’t envious. Reminding himself that phasing out of the industry life was his own decision, because that life only underlined all the things about him that made people not stick. Promising himself that once he really got used to it, and wasn’t so tired, he would start to find himself in this new role.

Chapter 7

Willem did get used to it eventually. Trained his voice for the hours of talking, memorized the usual spiel and the usual prompts for the group classes, memorized all the students' names. The process gave him new material for his AA meetings. He knew he wasn't the only one there who treated them as a sort of performance. He'd even discussed it once, with another long-timer who worked occasionally as an actor. It was like improv, they agreed. Making up a story on the spot. The facts had to be true, and the feelings, but that didn't mean they couldn't make it entertaining. It was very, very rare for Willem to let what he said veer toward sadness or fear or even anger. This was the place to talk about his addiction and how he was managing it. Nothing else. Nothing before.

The new work helped. It was constructive. Before long he got sufficiently friendly with the rest of the regular instructors that he could start to feel he was part of a company again. Not a cast, obviously; it would never be that, though he wasn't the only ex-dancer (sort of 'ex') in the place. But they were all working together toward a common goal, which was to draw good students who could and would pay for private lessons. That required a common standard of behavior (one quite different from what Willem was used to backstage) and occasionally some sharing. A student who didn't prosper in one class might do very well in another, simply due to the change of chemistry.

One of the regular instructors was a Korean man old enough to be Willem's father. Another was a woman who might have been thirty. Those two were good friends, and neither of them had side jobs. They were both at the yoga studio almost full-time, which meant Willem saw a lot of them. He quickly bonded with Karen, in particular. They were down the street at the coffee shop one day when she started complaining about her ballet class. Willem perked up. "You take ballet class?"

"I started back a year ago. Year and a half? I can't remember." She slurped her tea. "This guy came into my vinyasa class about two years ago. He was a dancer and he was having a mid-life crisis and I had to chuck him out because he was giving everyone else the jitters. I thought he might go to one of the other classes, that's what I told him to do, but he never came back. I feel a little guilty about it." She shrugged, looking guilty. "Anyway I also told him to find a different way to dance if what he was doing wasn't working for him, and then after the fact I thought, you miss it, go do it. So I found a class." She told him where it was. They were on their way back to Tidal Flow when she gave him a sideways look and said, "You want to come with me sometime?"

He took a minute to think about it. "I've been telling myself it's better to make a clean break. But I miss it. My body doesn't feel right without it. I couldn't get to that place on my bike though." He wondered why she didn't go to Set The Barre, which was in walking distance from Tidal Flow. Then he thought *maybe that guy works there* and dismissed it.

"I'll drive. I'll tell my cats I'm taking a hot dancer out and they'll give me that 'oh sure you are' look." Willem laughed. Karen sipped her tea, smiling. "I gripe about the class because the teacher makes me do things I don't want to do. Ironic, huh."

The first time at that class, Willem felt like he could suddenly breathe again. He shook hands with

Mandy, the owner-slash-instructor, and assured her he'd be back. She looked pleased, asking, "How long has it been?"

"Only since last fall, really." He told her about doing 'The Great Wave.'

Mandy's face lit up. "You were in that? I saw that! It was fantastic!"

"Hardest thing I've ever done," he admitted. "Going from that to a cruise-ship revue was, um, a little beyond stepping it down." She laughed. They shook hands and he turned to collect Karen.

She was waiting a few steps up the hall. "Again next week?"

"God, yes." In the car on the way home, he said, "I really had no idea *how much* I missed it."

"Well, you've been busy. How long were you a dancer?"

He had to think about it. When did he start taking lessons? "Jesus. Since I was six. Twenty-nine years."

"No wonder you missed it. I did it from five to twenty, basically. Had to stop in college, some personal stuff."

Willem took that to mean 'personal stuff I'd rather not go into right now or maybe ever,' which was fine. He had a lot of that himself. Things he didn't tell anybody, things he'd *never* told anybody. Things he could barely tolerate thinking of, much less speaking of. So whatever Karen's history was, he'd respect her boundaries. Something told him she would respect his too.

They got closer over the next few months, and if both of them knew it was primarily due to proximity, there was also a genuine attraction. They had dancing and yoga in common, plus a similarly practical approach to life. Karen was, and would always be, closer to Kevin; she and the older Korean instructor had something like a father-daughter relationship. But Kevin was married. Having a single friend was always good for a single Los Angeleno. Especially one who wasn't, for whatever reason, actively looking for love, which neither of them seemed to be doing.

After a while, perhaps inevitably, they began to talk about why they were single. Karen told Willem about a guy she'd dated for a while, who suggested they move in together, but without her cats. "That was the end of that," she said. "Like, immediately."

"Your cats are nice." He had one on his lap at that very moment. "You've had them forever. Why would he think you would give them up?"

"Gold-plated penis? I don't know." She managed to hold onto her cranky face until he stopped laughing. "It wasn't, by the way." He laughed again. She picked up her vintage porcelain teacup (she had several, mismatched, all from thrift shops) and sipped. "I realized I'm not sure what I want out of life, so I probably shouldn't be dating. But you're doing the life change thing. You must know what you want."

"I'm doing the midlife crisis thing, like your jittery guy." Willem took a minute, sipping his own tea, then setting the cup down to put both hands on the cat. "Ow, Gabbana, dude. No claws please. Why do they always puncture me when they're happy?"

"Well, they're cats. Come on."

He knew what she meant. "I met a guy last year. During the lead-up to that concert at Chrome. We dated for six weeks. Had exactly six dates. And then I left for the cruise thing."

"But."

He sighed. "But I thought we had something. Right from the start. He talked to me. He listened, and we laughed a lot. He was nothing like my usual, aside from being really good-looking." Karen snorted into her teacup. Willem shrugged. He couldn't apologize for dating good-looking guys. "I was crazy busy and I think I missed a lot, because what I mostly wanted to do was get him into bed."

"Which I assume you did." As if anything else was inconceivable.

"Three times. The first time was our first date, and the third time was our fifth date, and that time he let me stay over. I would swear he never does that."

"How old is he?"

"I don't know. My age, at least, I think."

"What kind of place does he have?"

"One-bedroom apartment in Mid City, near the County Museum of Art. He works in Century City, he's a records manager at a law firm."

"Oh wow, a manager. Where did you meet him?"

"Here's the crazy part." Willem was gazing at her, but he wasn't really seeing her. He was seeing Richard again, on the other side of the crowded dance studio, remembering that moment like a scene from a movie. All the chatter and commotion fading out when they made eye contact, as if recognizing each other: oh, it's you; I've been waiting. "He's a dancer. Ballroom dancer. He was at Shall We Dance last summer when we started full-cast rehearsals for 'The Great Wave.' I don't know what happened."

You fell in love, she thought and didn't say. Instead she petted Dolce and sipped her tea. "But you haven't seen him since?"

"Our sixth date was closing night. He came with me to the show, and I thought … well, I hoped we would spend the night together again. But he left during the after-party and he didn't even text me. I was dancing with somebody, we were all a little crazy, and the next thing I knew he was gone." After a minute, eyes on the cat, he said, "I should have called him. I can't stand not knowing why." Karen reached over from the other chair, patted his shoulder, and changed the subject.

Willem finally caught up with Dexter's Underground Cabaret performance in April. Then he went down the rabbit hole, watching all the numbers he could find online that had been posted since 'The Great Wave.' He honestly didn't know what else was happening on dance stages around town, but he couldn't imagine much of it being more interesting than what was happening with this company. He wondered if Dexter planned to do anything else with them, after the arc on 'Ten-31' was finished.

There were a few more posts from Richard, linking to some of those Cabaret performances. He seemed to have been in a show-runner capacity for the March event. One of the performers –a salsa champion who'd begun doing the Cabaret with her partner the year before – posted a picture of herself with Richard. She was wearing a brief theater-arts costume in black and red, calling to mind a roulette wheel. He was wearing a crimson velvet evening jacket and was smiling at her. He looked spectacular. His status was still 'single.'

Chapter 8

May 2017

Everyone at Shall We Dance was slowly getting back to normal. The front of the studio was repaired, the horrible stain on the sidewalk long since scrubbed away. Dmitri never set up the café tables and chairs he usually put out there in the spring. Most of the regulars still avoided the front, coming in through the back. But the place was busy, because all the competitors were still in training. All except Julia, who'd never returned after losing Ray in the accident.

After a couple of rough and overworked months, and several interviews, Dmitri filled the gap by hiring a past world Latin champion. Hiro Miyazaki had most recently been teaching in San Diego; before that, London. His resumé was unbeatable. He was also tall, straight, and movie-star handsome. All of a sudden the studio was flooded with new female students. Everyone involved – including Hiro – thought it was funny. Mateo had a personal interest in it: his sister.

"Kris is after him," he told Richard at dinner one night. "She was at the studio the day he interviewed and she was like, mine." Richard laughed. Mateo made a 'yeah, for real' face. "After the first-look for the pro show they went to dinner and, you know, I'm proud of her."

"What happened?" Richard thought he could guess.

"Banged him, like all night, and got the first two marriage proposals out of the way." Mateo had already laughed about this for roughly an hour, so he managed to not crack up, simply grinning while he waited for

Richard to compose himself. Sam had laughed a lot too when he heard about it. "So you finished your DVIDA shit, right?"

Richard nodded, swallowed some wine, and said, "I mentioned to Dmitri that I'd like to be considered for the evening group classes. Not yours," he assured Mateo. "But the other three."

Mateo thought this was a fantastic idea. "It would be great to have you onboard. Did you get any sense he'd go for it?"

"He said we would talk after 'Face the Music.' I feel like I could be helpful while that's going on, but he's so much less stressed now that Hiro's in the house. You're all back in the groove." Richard changed the subject. "I loved seeing Sam's thing at the showcase last month. You're doing yours this time, right? From the tango show?"

"My solo from 'Gaucho,' right. And we have something else happening. I don't know if Rory told you." Mateo had been holding onto this news with difficulty. "Sam and I are getting married."

"Mateo! That's wonderful!" Richard was out of his seat.

Mateo stood up too and they hugged hard. When they separated and sat down again he had to wipe his eyes. "I'm doing this all the time, so soggy. I've wanted to marry him for so long, and we never really said those words to each other until Kris fell in love, and then I said I want to call you my husband. And he said I want that too. So we're doing it in Rory and Dana's yard."

"And then you're traveling for competition, and doing another new dance for 'Cosmic,' and starring in 'Face the Music.' I'm guessing there will not really be a honeymoon, per se."

Mateo giggled. "Not exactly, no. Not for a while. Eh, who needs a honeymoon."

"Maybe at the end of the year," Richard said. "Things are usually quieter in December."

"Yeah, maybe. So aside from finishing up your certification, what's new with you? Didn't Paula throw you at this guy in her office who does your job?"

Richard dipped his head, hiding a smile. "She did. He was nice, and at least we had plenty to talk about."

"Did you bang him?"

"Jeez, Mateo! Well, yeah." Mateo laughed. Richard was still smiling, head up. "I haven't done that with anybody for a while. It was fine."

"But not something to run with."

"I don't think so, no. We had coffee a week after, and it was all, I like you but maybe that was enough. On both sides." Richard studied his plate, rearranged things again, had another bite. "It was good. Good to have that experience and not have it get weird on me."

Mateo wanted to ask if Richard was in touch with Willem at all. He knew the guy was in town, had a regular job, and was still allegedly single. But he left it alone. At least Richard was dating. "Sam's assistant and his wife are pregnant. I'm like oh great, now it's going to be even harder to get him to work nights. So Sam's training this girl who started last year on the opening and closing shit. I shouldn't call her a girl, she's like forty. I swear the first time I saw her I thought she was a guy. She has this 1930s lounge lizard thing going, it's totally dope."

"Is she an actress?"

"Honestly I have no idea, I've barely spoken to her." Mateo polished off his dinner. "But if we ever manage to get our shit together for Cicada again, we should take her along. God knows if she can dance but she looks perfect."

Richard got his phone out and opened up his calendar. "Maybe in October?"

"Fuck me, is that the first available?" Richard gave him a look. Mateo cracked up again. "I know, I know!" He got his phone out too. "Okay. It's in the calendar. Now can I tell you my secret plan for the wedding?"

"God, yes. Something Sam doesn't know about?"

"Totally." Mateo looked gleeful as he told Richard all about the full-on geisha drag look he was working on. Richard listened, smiling, glad to have friends like these. Maybe he'd reached out at exactly the right moment for all of them.

July 2017

Willem was in a groove. Steady work, which by its nature was never exactly the same from one day to the next. The vinyasa classes designed by Rhonda were set in stone, but every group of students was different. The content of his own class changed every six weeks, and he could do whatever he (or his clients) wanted in private sessions. He and Karen were still getting along great; he and Mandy had progressed to active friendship. The ballet class was another source of students. None of it added up to the excitement of preparing for a show, but on the other hand he was making good money and spending hardly anything.

When the Emmy nominations were announced, he was paying attention. Dexter's guest role on 'Ten-31' had gotten a lot of buzz; Willem had his fingers crossed. He was at Tidal Flow, prepping for an early class, when the news posted. "Hot damn," he said out loud, and immediately sent a text: *Congratulations! I guess you'd better propose to Rita now*

He didn't get a reply till the end of the day, which wasn't surprising. Dexter was busy filming a rom-com for Netflix. When the text did roll in it made Willem laugh: *Uh yeah about that I kind of already did. We were thinking September for the wedding but now it'll probably be December*

Yeah those two things in one month would be crazy. Really awesome dude, happy for you all around

Thanks buddy! Let's get together soon, I haven't seen you forever

Meet up at Barneys for old time's sake?

OMG LOL no. How about Sisley

Willem rolled his eyes. Sisley was over the hill, in the Valley. An Uber would get him there and back, but still. *Earth to TV star, still on two wheels, how about Javier's instead*

That works, ping me a few possible dates and we'll make it happen. Willem acknowledged, disconnected, and thought about everything that had gone right for Dexter in the past year. He could freely admit, in the privacy of his own brain, that he was envious. That rom-com had to be hella fun to work on. It was about a college production of 'Anything Goes.' Dexter was playing the out-of-town tap expert helping the faculty advisor. Of course they fell in love. And they were only the secondary couple, the stars both played college students, but Dexter was getting a big tap number.

Willem examined the envy for a minute. It wasn't the acting success, so much, although there was a little of that because he knew perfectly well what kind of money went with it. It was having a featured dance role like that. And having a lover, a fiancée, to come home to. It was time he stopped pretending he was too busy to date. Time to think about where he could meet someone. Not someone to fuck, because that was always easy. He wanted a lover. He wanted a relationship. He wanted someone like Richard, if not the man himself.

He wasn't sure he was brave enough. But he could at least dip a toe in the water. Get a look at the guy again. The first time they saw each other they'd both been interested. Maybe the break had been long enough that Richard would be interested again. And if not, at least Willem could meet some new people. He'd go to the summer pro show. Maybe he'd get inspired, and maybe … well, maybe.

September 2017

"Yes," Richard said, managing his breath with difficulty. "I'd love to. Thank you." He and Dmitri shook hands. They talked for a few more minutes, about when Richard would take over the evening group classes and the Sunday morning Cardio Latin class. They also discussed which of the Saturday socials he would prefer to host: first, second, or third weekend. They agreed to leave that up to fate. The other hosts were Mateo and Hiro, both of whom were apt to have competition or show obligations. Richard didn't expect to. He could take whichever night didn't work for the others.

This had been a possibility since February. Since everyone knew Julia wasn't coming back. By the time Richard had spoken to Dmitri about the possibility, he was looking his age – nearly sixty – for the first time, tired and careworn. He'd been trying to accommodate all the private students. It was impossible; there simply weren't enough hours in the day. Now, four full months into the new paradigm, Dmitri looked rested. Hiro was a terrific asset for the studio. Bringing him in had been like mounting a neon sign in front. And he was imminently marrying Mateo's sister Kristine. Mateo would have been completely giddy about that if he'd had any giddy left over from his own wedding.

When Richard went in to do the paperwork with Elena she said, "Thank you. Thank you for doing the work, thank you for being so steady all these years, thank you for choosing the right moment. I was really getting worried about the boss."

"We all were," he said, after making sure the door was closed.

"And thank you for stepping up with Mating Dance. We didn't know how the hell we were going to manage that on top of our campaigns." Elena was gunning for an Open Professional Rhythm title with Mateo; Dmitri's former partner was planning to debut in Rising Star Smooth with a new partner in November. Hiro hadn't yet decided about a new competitive campaign, but Richard thought it was only a matter of time. With three out of four full-time staffers competing, having coverage for the four evening group classes was highly desirable. He'd be saving the others a world of anxiety, not to mention paperwork. Mateo ordinarily taught the social Rhythm class on Tuesdays, and would continue unless he was traveling with Elena. The others had all been pitching in. None of them would have to work those extra hours anymore.

Richard still thought he could have started earlier in the summer, but the studio had already coped with two big changes this year. He understood. "I almost told Dmitri if the studio wasn't doing so well, staffing it wouldn't have been a problem. After all these years I never quite know if he knows I'm joking."

"None of us do," Elena assured him. "The guy has the original poker face. Anyway, I remember when it was just him. This is better. Patrick must be so happy." Dmitri's husband had been patient for a very long time, waiting for the studio to stop consuming ninety percent of Dmitri's waking hours. "But what about you? You're still keeping your day job, right?"

"Of course." Richard was sitting in one of the guest chairs, wondering how it would feel when he was on the other side of the desk. A part of the studio at last, after all those years of study and practice and testing.

Maybe Elena saw that. "You should sit over here. And you should know we have the passwords and shit written down. I know everyone says don't do that, but even Patrick says don't worry about it." They changed places. Elena showed him where to find the schedule, the contacts list, the instructors' notes. A lot of independents had teaching privileges at Shall We Dance, but they all had to arrange floor time in advance. Obviously there wouldn't be any private lessons happening during group classes, but Richard could expect to get messages in the evening. Instructors would be trying to reserve time.

"So it'll be up to me whether I give them an hour?" Richard was smiling.

So was Elena. "Don't let it go to your head. All of these people have been in and out of here for a long time."

"I know. Dmitri's careful about who he lets in." Which made this new position feel like even more of a reward. "Having this to look forward to is going to make the records room a lot less boring."

Elena perched on the edge of the desk. "When did you decide you wanted to do the teacher training?"

"Oh, a long time ago. I needed an excuse to keep coming, after doing the group classes so many times. I didn't want to do competition, I'm not up to it physically, but I can do a couple hours a night at the pace of a group class."

"Why do you say you're not up to it? I've seen you dancing with Mateo or Sam, or Mike, or whoever. I've danced with you. You hold your own."

Richard decided it was time she knew. Elena had been with the studio five years. They were officially co-workers now. "I've had an eating disorder for going on twenty years. It's done some damage. My doctors always said be careful." He wouldn't mention the training he'd been doing with the jazz dancers. He still wasn't sure that amounted to any more than performance-adjacent fun. Never mind that Mateo had said 'one of these days we'll get you back on stage.' The thought made him smile again. "Your partner is an instigator."

"My partner is a lunatic," Elena said, tone full of exasperated affection. "Did he tell you what we're doing in November?"

Richard was still smiling. "He said you're doing 'Mamboscope' with your competition mambo but turned up to eleven."

"Yeah, basically. You know we did some tricks last year for our show dance, and of course Mateo says we have to top that this year." She rolled her eyes. "We've spent six hours with Michelle. Six hours! She's all, this is how you do this lift. I'm all, you are out of your mind." Richard laughed. "He makes it work somehow. He's strong as an ox."

"I remember. When we did our paso he had me in the air a few times."

"I saw that. I did a complete Cabaret binge after starting here. Michelle said, watch these DVDs. Told me I was going to see a lot of crazy shit on the floor, this place isn't always strictly ballroom, and boy was she right."

"I love it," he said softly. "Something new every month, but so many of the same people. And such great performances. I remember the first time I saw Michelle dance with Vince."

"Oh my *God.*" Elena remembered that too; that was before she came crawling back to Dmitri, before he and Michelle were even training as partners. "That was *so hot*. She says, we couldn't stop thinking for even a second. She said when they looked at the video later and realized it came off it was like, whew. That's my official goal with 'Mamboscope.' If there's anybody in the club who doesn't know us, to make them think Mateo and I are banging."

Richard laughed. "You're always hot together though." Elena looked pleased. "And it's time for you to get home. I promise not to delete anything out of here." He indicated the computer. She laughed, got her stuff together, kissed his cheek, and left. Richard stayed there for another half hour, getting familiar with the studio's records. He could tell already that his work experience was going to be more helpful here than he'd thought.

And this was another piece of the puzzle notching into place. Over the past year he had somehow gone from a mere satellite of the Shall We Dance community to an integral part of it. He was healthier than he'd been in twenty years, he liked himself more than he ever had, and the last few dates he'd been on told him other people liked him too. He'd even been to bed with Paula's friend, and the experience hadn't triggered anything. Maybe he was finally ready to address that big What If.

What if the reason Willem came back to Los Angeles, stayed and put down roots, was because of him? He couldn't help wondering. Willem could have gone anywhere after that cruise gig, but he came back and went to work at that yoga studio. Richard couldn't help noticing that if Willem was dating at all, he wasn't posting about it. There were pictures of him at a ballet class, and with one of his co-workers. His status was 'single.'

They'd missed each other once, at Chrome. The summer pro show this year was huge, with sixteen numbers and eighteen dancers. It seemed as though everybody in Los Angeles who had the slightest interest in dancing had gone to see it. Richard went to closing night, which was standing room only.

He heard after the fact, from Mateo, that Willem was there on opening night. They were both at the studio, sitting in chairs along the wall, watching some competitors practice. "You should have been in the show this summer," Mateo said. "You could have done any of those group numbers. Then that fucker would have seen you up on stage and thought, well hell, there's the one that got away."

It made Richard laugh. It was technically true that he could have done the group numbers this time. 'Face the Music' was a ballroom-heavy show, unlike 'The Great Wave.' But everyone else in the cast was well-known to the audience who came to the dance shows at Chrome. Richard didn't have the same recognition factor. Plus, "Alison was not going to plug me in instead of you or Hiro or Vince, or Dmitri for God's sake. You all have actual fan clubs."

"You could have a fan club too." Mateo did that thing, leaning in to nudge Richard with his shoulder. "Sexy motherfucker."

Richard nudged back. "Speak for yourself. I can't wait to see you and Sam dancing in 'Milonga.'" They were bringing back a number from the 2015 pro show, even though Mateo and Elena were traveling to Hawaii that month for a competition. "We've got a lot of new couples in the show but the comments say everyone's coming to see you."

"No they don't and no they are not." Mateo was delighted. "Not with fucking Hiro in the show." Dmitri's new Latin expert had taken the L.A. ballroom community by storm, and this was his first time doing a number with the Cabaret. "Speaking of fucking Hiro, I wish you had come to the wedding."

"Somebody needed to keep the studio open. All of you slackers were in Temecula." Richard had actually taken a vacation day from the law office and spent it in West Hollywood so the rest of the staff could go to Hiro and Kristine's wedding. "So many weddings this year."

"Yeah. Well." They both knew why. After losing Ray, people had looked around and thought, now. First Sam and Mateo, then Rory and Dana. All said 'we should have done this before.' Mateo gave Richard a sideways glance. "Kristine's pregnant."

"Jeez, already?"

"If you'd been there opening night you wouldn't wonder. He totally banged her in the green room."

"He did not! There's no lock on the door!"

Mateo nodded. "Did it in the bathroom. She was like, hottest thing ever. I was like, are you a gay guy in disguise?"

November 2017

There were a lot of good reasons for Richard to be at Chrome for both nights of 'Mating Dance: Mamboscope.' Mateo and Elena were performing their tricked-out show dance, and two other couples from Shall We Dance would take the stage. Another nine performances came from all over the city. Richard took some pride in the fact that their casting notices got such a good response, after all these years. It would have been dangerously easy to let Shall We Dance dominate all of the productions.

He was also proud of the show design. The performers all chose their own music and did their own choreography. It was the show runner's responsibility to set the order of performance, creating a sequence that would work for the audience. They weren't trying to tell a story; it was more a matter of making sure the mood and tempo and style of the music had a good flow. Kind of like being a DJ, with the added challenge of the visual component. This time, he had longtime Cabaret stars Vince and Kelli opening Act One with a traditional mambo set to a 1950s-era classic. Mateo and Elena closed Act One with their longer, tricktastic show dance. Anya and Ricky, a pro salsa couple who always had some amazing stunts in their routines, would be closing Act Two.

There was an extra buzz in the club tonight. Richard wasn't sure if it was because of the friends-and-family after-party, or something else. He couldn't help noticing that Anya's boyfriend Terry wasn't tending bar tonight. He was dressed to kill, providing a semi-managerial presence but looking awfully distracted. Like he had a very enjoyable secret.

Richard dismissed the question after the Act One curtain call. During intermission, when the first group of performers were making their way out from backstage to the house, he did some handshakes and hugs. Then he went backstage himself for a minute to check in with Rory, who was stage-managing. She told him everything was fine and to get out of her way. He obediently left the stage and headed for the bar.

Chapter 9

Willem came to see 'Mamboscope,' finding a seat in the mezzanine lounge. He wasn't invited to the after-party, so he figured he'd get a head start out the door by staying upstairs. Then he saw Richard leaving the stage. The next thing he knew, he was down the stairs and looking for that peacock-blue velvet evening jacket. Richard had never worn anything like that when they were dating, but his more recent posts were full of it. Rich colors and soft textures. Willem couldn't help wondering who was touching them. Richard's status was still 'single,' and he never posted a picture with another man who looked like a date.

He was collecting a drink from the bartender when Willem fetched up beside him, opened his mouth, and couldn't think of anything to say. Richard turned and saw him. "Oh. Hi Willem."

"Hi." It was all he could manage. Richard looked phenomenal. He always had, but tonight he looked strong and happy and … younger. Taller. And sexy. Under the close-fitting velvet jacket was a silky shirt the color of an oil slick. Dark bronze and iridescent. It had to be a dancewear fabric. "God, you look amazing."

Richard did that thing he always did, turning his head a few degrees and averting his eyes, as if the smile got away from him. "Thank you." He looked up again, making eye contact. "It's good to see you too. I owe you an apology."

Willem's eyebrows shot up. That was the last thing he expected. "You do?"

"I shouldn't have left without saying anything. Last year, I mean, at 'The Great Wave.' I needed to leave, but I should have found you and said something. I'm sorry."

"It's okay." Willem would have sworn he was still mad about that, but suddenly it didn't seem to matter anymore. Saying 'I wanted to spend the night with you' now struck him as both pointless and crass. Richard didn't owe him anything, then or now. "Um. I'm glad I caught you. To say hi."

"Yes. I'm glad too." Richard wanted to say more, wanted very badly to say something more personal, but he wasn't really prepared for this. He needed a script. Since he didn't have one, he defaulted to business. "I'm kind of on duty at the moment, but maybe we could talk later?"

"After the show?" Willem had a class to teach at nine in the morning, but he could do that in his sleep by now. "I wasn't invited to the after-party."

"Hang on." Richard set his glass on the bar. "I'll be right back." He worked his way through the crowd to the stairs. Willem watched him go, noticing the black cowboy boots under the black tuxedo pants. *That's why he looked taller*. It made him smile, even though he felt very iffy about Richard walking away right at this moment. Where the hell was he going?

When the bartender asked if she could get him anything, Willem requested a Pellegrino. He was paying for it when Richard got back to him, a gold wristband in one hand and a miniature pair of scissors in the other. Without asking, he wrapped the band around Willem's wrist, snapped it closed, and cut off the trailing end. The lights dimmed. "Just in time." He looked up at Willem again, almost smiling. Then he reached over for his drink, drained the glass, winced as though he hadn't expected it to be quite so alcoholic, set the glass back on the bar, and turned away.

Willem couldn't believe it. Not another word? An apology, an assumption that Willem could and would stay, an unsolicited wristband, a quick exit. What the fuck did all that add up to? He watched Richard cross the room again and go up the stage steps. Oh. He really was on duty. Of course he was. He was running these shows now. He had to make sure all the performers were there, make sure the stage manager had the music and knew all the cues. Willem told himself to watch, to pay attention to the performances. He knew some of these people, after all. Dexter kept telling him he should audition. It would certainly be one way to keep seeing Richard.

Except he honestly couldn't tell if Richard had any remaining interest in him. Maybe he should leave it alone. Have a few words with him, make a point of talking to the performers, then get out. That was definitely what he should do. He needed time to think about this.

He wished there was someone else here, *anyone* else, he could talk to. Should've invited Karen. He'd tell her about it later, unless this turned out to be nothing more than are we cool, good, have a nice life.

Backstage, Richard closed his eyes for a moment to enjoy the memory of Willem's face after he finished with the wristband. Startled, confused, and as if he'd just won something. Maybe there was hope after all. He took a breath and went to talk to Rory.

The second half went great. Richard would have sworn he wasn't deliberately looking for Willem during the last number, but somehow he knew exactly where the other man was. Then he saw Terry, going up the stage steps while Ricky and Anya were in their ending position. He was behind Anya so she couldn't see him, but Ricky could. A flash of delight crossed Ricky's face and he held position, keeping Anya down until Terry was there to take his place. He let her stand up; he got down on one knee; he proposed. There was no doubt about it, even though not many people could have possibly heard him. And then Anya shushed the audience. She asked them if she should say yes, and of course everyone said she should. It was stupid, and hilarious, and awesome. Richard turned his head and made eye contact with Willem, who must have already been looking at him. *Oh Lord*, Richard thought. What did that look mean? They weren't even dating. They were more than a year into not-dating. He took a couple of deep breaths, still watching Willem, trying not to let his face say anything it shouldn't.

Willem kept telling himself he was only staying so he could play nice with all these Mating Dance people. Pass out some business cards, congratulate the performers, maybe have a few minutes of actual conversation with the stage manager. Maybe it was one of the same people from the year before. And maybe he'd have another word or two with Richard. But the guy knew where to find him. Willem had made the first move tonight, as he had before. An apology and a wristband didn't add up to 'let's go to bed' or anything else.

Then the show was over, and there was that proposal happening on stage, and the next thing he knew he was staring at Richard. Their gazes locked. Willem felt pinned in place. The Chrome staff began subtly steering people toward the stairs – people who didn't have those golden-ticket wristbands – and Richard was approaching. He looked wary again, as if maybe he'd been thinking of reasons why he shouldn't talk to Willem. Why the apology was a good place to leave it. When he was standing right there, Willem lost his head. “I’m going to a friend’s wedding on December third. They said I could bring a date. Do you want to go with me?”

Richard blinked, inhaled, and said, “Yes.” They stared at each other for a moment. Willem had a bottle of Pellegrino in his hand. Richard took note of that, took note of his expression: again startled, again confused, but this time as if he wished they were alone. Richard definitely did. But they weren’t there yet, and they both had to know it. He said, “Let me introduce you to the cast.” Willem nodded, and they started to mingle.

He knew Mateo and Sam, of course, from their show together. Took note of the way they leaned on each other, and their wedding rings. Instead of mentioning that he said, “Do you ever watch our show and think damn, didn’t know I could do that? Because I do.”

Mateo gave a big-eyed nod. “I’d been working with Sam on some of the martial-arts stuff for years, but we went places none of us expected with those characters.”

“You’re both really great,” Willem said, with rueful honesty. “I’ve been wishing ever since that I had a chance to do something like that earlier.”

“What are you doing now?”

He told them about transitioning to yoga teacher. Richard stood close, listening with apparent interest. Willem didn’t go on about it very long; he could tell the other men had a lot of people to talk to. Once they’d gone, he told Richard he had to teach in the morning. “So I should probably go. You’ve probably got an early start too.”

"Yes, I do. But I like to spend a little time talking to people after these things. It helps keep the connection strong." That wasn't intended to sound personal, but they both heard it that way. "Do you still have my number?"

"Yes I do. I'll send you the details on that thing." For some reason, Willem didn't want to say 'wedding' again. He offered a hand. Richard took it with a slight smile, squeezed gently, then let him go.

Willem was still thinking about it when he got home, and the next morning. He thought he'd better warn Dexter, so he sent a text before heading to Tidal Flow: *Hey buddy I managed to get a date for your big day. He will be dressed better than me*

The response came back right before Willem went into the vinyasa room: *As long as he isn't dressed better than ME*

No guarantees sorry

LOL whatever see you there! Willem put his phone away. Half of him was glad his friend had so much good shit going on right now, the way half of him was happy for Sam and Mateo. The other half was trying to ignore the voice that kept telling him he'd never have anything like that. He'd never even have the chance, because the whole world knew he didn't have what it took. He wasn't steady enough, successful enough, good enough.

The worst part of being an alcoholic was knowing the addiction was a liar and believing it anyway.

At a meeting later that week, he asked, "Has anyone gone through one of those periods where it seems like everyone around you is getting married?" Of course nearly everyone had, though mostly in their twenties. After a few people had told their stories, talking about how weddings were hell on sobriety, Willem said, "I've never been in that place with someone. I mean the long-term commitment place. My experience with weddings is basically terrible. But now I'm going to one and, you know, let's talk about strategies for avoiding the champagne."

"How good is this friend?"

"Do you have to go?"

"Is he going to give you any shit about not drinking?"

"Who else will be there?"

Willem fielded all the questions. "We've known each other a long time and worked together. Yes, I have to go. I *want* to go. He won't give me any shit about drinking. I have no idea who all will be there, but there'll probably be other people I've worked with." He paused. Weddings really were hell on sobriety. "I guess the best thing to do is keep a glass of ginger ale in my hand at all times."

People mostly agreed with that. "Unless you get a chance to dance," someone said. "I love dancing at weddings. The bar is so low. So to speak."

Everyone laughed. Then another person said, "The alternative is to explain yourself continuously, all night, to people who don't really have a right to know about your issues."

"Yeah." Willem heaved a sigh. "Well, enough about me. Who else has a holiday thing coming up that looks like hell in a handbasket?" That turned into a discussion of office parties and what a nightmare they were. Willem didn't have to speak again before the meeting wrapped up.

He told his siblings about it too, in a roundabout way, over the course of a three-way phone call about the holidays. His sister Stephanie wanted to know about the last wedding he went to. “Yours,” he said. “I haven’t been around people who were getting married or who would’ve asked me to come if they were.”

“Well, it’s good that you’re closer to some people now,” she said. “How’s the career change going?”

“Pretty good! I’ve made a friend there, too.” He seized the opportunity to tell them all about Karen, and going to ballet class, and the other normal stuff in his life. It was actually really nice to run all that down, as if to confirm he was getting somewhere, finally. He didn’t tell them about Richard, though.

Chapter 10

Richard had been strongly tempted to mention Willem to Rory backstage at 'Mamboscope.' He knew she saw them together at the after-party. There was no way she wasn't going to demand some kind of update. So after he got to work and had everything organized for the day, he went in his office and sent a text: *Hi Rory, did you notice Willem was at Chrome last night?*

The answer was immediate: *Uh yeah. So?*

I apologized for walking out on him last year

And?

He asked me to come to a friend's wedding on the third. I said yes

Well that's interesting

LOL yes. Richard debated for a second, then added: *I don't think he meant to ask me*

Till he saw you lookin fly

He laughed for a minute, stifling it so his clerks wouldn't hear. *Maybe*

So where is the thing and who's getting married?

I don't even know, he said he would send me the info

Bitch please! It might be in Bali!

LMAO I think he would have mentioned that

Wait a minute that date. We're going to a wedding. Dexter Parker and Rita Johnson. If it's the same one tell me immediately so I can start scheming

NO SCHEMING this will happen or it won't

Gaahh no fun. Get to work OXO

TTYL OXO. Richard put the phone away, wondering what the odds were. If it turned out to be the same event, Willem might be in for an interrogation.

At the end of the day, he got a message from the man himself. He still couldn't imagine what the odds were, but it was the same event Rory and Dana were going to. He sent a note to Rory to let her know, sent a confirmation to Willem, hesitated, then added a postscript asking if he could pick Willem up. By now the other man might have his own car, but then again he might not. There were a lot of good reasons not to have a car.

Willem got that note and said "Fuck" out loud, which made Karen laugh. He was in her car, on the way to their ballet class. He gave her an apologetic look and said, "I invited this guy to that wedding, and he asked if I wanted him to drive, and now I feel like a loser."

"Don't be ridiculous," she said crisply. "It is stupid expensive to have a car, especially in Los Angeles, and all they are most of the time is a pain in the patootie. If it really pinches your ego, rent one for the day. But you have a good reason not to have a car, so if you ask me, which you didn't, just say yes."

"It's that same guy, though. The one from last year. I couldn't help feeling my overall failure at adulting was one reason he walked."

Karen took a moment, because this was kind of momentous news. "Did he say so?"

"Well … no. I didn't ask," he admitted. "I didn't contact him at all after that, until literally yesterday. I went to that thing at Chrome, and he was there, and I teleported from the mezzanine to the downstairs bar and then couldn't say anything."

Oh honey. Karen almost laughed. "So he said something? What did he say?"

"He apologized for bailing. He didn't say why he did, and once more I didn't ask." He was exasperated with himself about it. No doubt that came through in his tone, even though he remembered how it seemed unimportant when they were face to face.

"Does it matter?"

Willem had to think about that for a minute. "I don't know. I mean, I had that contract. I was leaving the next day."

"Well, maybe that's why. If he really liked you and you were going to be gone for months, maybe he thought it was best to do a fade." Karen's tone was so reasonable that Willem almost accepted that. Whatever, it was history, and this was something new. He was still thinking about it when they parked at the ballet studio. Then he had to get his head in the game. After class, Karen was in the mood to discuss what they were doing. Willem couldn't start obsessing about Richard again until she dropped him off at home.

"One of these days I'll figure out a way to pay you back for all this," he said. She frowned at him. "Come on, it's not exactly on your way."

"It's not exactly not, either. Don't worry about it. I like having a ballet buddy. See you at work."

"See you." He watched her drive away, wondered what he was going to eat, remembered he had a few things in his mini fridge. *I need to finish growing up.* He let himself in through the back door, as usual, and went straight to his room. The first thing he did after eating was write back to Richard: *Thanks, I'm still on two wheels so we'll probably be more comfortable in your car.* Then he sat down with his laptop and his box of files to figure out how close he was to being in shape for getting his own place. It didn't have to be much. But it needed to be his.

Richard Googled the wedding couple after he got home. They obviously weren't connected to Shall We Dance, but on the other hand they were connected to Dana and Rory, so the odds were good they would have some kind of online presence. The things he dug up made him shake his head: he'd seen Dexter Parker, not once but three times. He should have remembered the name. *Give yourself a break*. There had been a lot going on this year. Dexter had danced with the Cabaret in February, and then he'd been on 'Ten-31' in that storyline the show came up with to cover the loss of Ray Daniels. Which, of course, was Dana's show too. That was undoubtedly how she'd come to know the guy. And then there was that Netflix movie about the college production of 'Anything Goes.' It had been released only a couple of weeks ago. Dexter was great in that. It was actually really cool that Richard was going to his wedding, and would have a chance to greet the man and say 'you were great.' His fiancée worked at a casting agency. She was beautiful. Their 'our story' essay told about how Dexter worked as an extra for a lot of years, and Rita was a background coordinator, and finally he asked her to dinner. The rest, as they said, was history.

Richard now had to think about a gift. He found their registry, which was one of the easy ones: basically no tangible things requested, and a statement to the effect that having their friends and family with them was all they needed, but that if people felt compelled to give something, there was a honeymoon fund. Richard was perfectly happy to contribute to that. Then he started thinking about what to wear to a church wedding held in the afternoon. He'd never been to such a thing. His initial thought was to go conservative, but – church notwithstanding – this was an Industry wedding, so maybe he could get away with something in his new style. He laid out the outfit he wanted to wear – his heather jacket, black chinos, and fake-snake boots with a white dress shirt and purple tie – took a phone picture, and sent it to Sam with a note: *Okay for afternoon church wedding of two Hollywood people? Dexter Parker and Rita Johnson.* He knew Sam would look them up. Would see that they were both African American, would see that Dexter and Dana had worked together, and would be able to render judgement accordingly.

The reply came back promptly: *Almost perfect. Swap in the lavender silk shirt and lose the tie*

LOL okay Obi-wan. Richard wondered how Willem would like the outfit. He had definitely liked the peacock jacket. He'd even touched it, more than once, mentioning the velvet in a half-apologetic way. As if Richard might've objected to being touched.

"It feels like forever since I've been touched," Richard told Rory on the phone later that week.

"Well," she said, "that's probably because it's *been* fucking forever. You were doing good with dating for a minute there. What happened?"

"I, uh." The truth was, he didn't have much of an excuse. "I might've been telling myself that running the classes and doing other stuff at the studio constituted a social life. And, I mean, dancing with people. That's contact. That's social."

Rory produced an unconvinced sound. "Yes, but it's pretty much the opposite of dating, since you're now part of the studio which means picking people up there is a no go. Talk to me."

"I *am* talking to you."

"Have you had dinner?"

"Fixing it right now, I promise."

"Good. Talk to me."

Richard laughed. "Okay, fine. I'm touch-hungry because Willem came downstairs to talk to me and ever since then all I can think about is the sex we had. And I've been dodging dates because I've been following him and there's no sign he's seeing anybody, and, you know, maybe there's a chance. Maybe we really could start over."

"Hmm. Do you want to start over, or do you want to start again? Because your actual start wasn't bad, was it?"

"No, it was great. I guess I'd like to build on that, if we can."

"Well, he did ask you to a wedding."

Her tone was so dry, Richard laughed again. "Yeah. I guess I have to wait to see what happens. Just really, you know, *impatient* all of a sudden. Anyway, what are you and Dana wearing to this thing?" He continued to assemble his dinner while Rory told him all about the fancier-than-usual outfits they had planned.

"I'm sorry," Willem said. "This should not be such a challenge to me. I'm freaking out about this wedding."

Karen stared at him over the rim of her travel mug. They were in the teachers' lounge, finishing their lunch, taking a break before going to their next classes. "Related to your transportation issue?"

He sighed. "I'll buy you dinner tonight if you come back to my place and help me figure out what to wear."

"Deal. You, sir, are a mess."

"I know!" He leaned over to kiss her cheek. "Thank you. I should be better at this. I've been to a million weddings." Mostly a long time ago, but whatever.

"Yeah, me too, but it's different when you're taking someone important." She patted his back, sighed, said, "Back to work," and went out without noticing his reaction. Willem thought, *Oh God, that's it, he's important and I don't know what to do*. He took a few minutes to sit with his eyes closed, deliberately thinking only of the class he'd be leading next, grateful that this job required focus.

There was a Thai restaurant in walking distance from where he lived. It wasn't the first time he and Karen met up there. She told stories about the last few weddings she'd been to – one of them their colleague Kevin's – while they ate. Then he hitched a ride back to his landlady's house. "You can park in the driveway," he said. "She told me she's not going anywhere tonight."

"Coolio. Let's go see what you have to work with."

"It's not much," he warned her.

For the first few minutes she seemed to agree, flipping through the things hanging in his closet. "You know, sweetie, there is minimal and then there is minimal." He snorted. She came to the garment bag squeezed into the back corner. "What's in here?"

"Oh shit, I forgot about that."

She gave him a sharp look and pulled it out, hooking the hanger over the rod in front of her, pulling down the zipper. "Is it a tux? That might be a little much for an afternoon wedding. Oh *hello*." She gazed at the beautiful silk suit. “That is gorgeous! When did you wear that?” She fingered the narrow black trousers, admired the mandarin-collared jacket in pearly blue, and turned to look at him.

“My brother married a Vietnamese girl,” he said. “They both wanted a South Asian style wedding. Silk and orchids and whatever everywhere.” He pulled out his phone and retrieved a photo, still in memory after five years because it made him happy to see it. “All of us wore those.”

“Oh my goodness. A couple of those guys … they must have been really good friends.” They both snickered. The style did not flatter everyone. “You looked amazing, though. You should wear this.”

“It’s not too fancy?” He kind of wanted to, though. He knew Richard would like it. And he hadn’t worn it since his sister’s wedding. He said so before he remembered what wasn’t great about that.

Karen didn’t miss his change of expression. “Uh, Willem.”

“Mmm?” He pretended to be looking for the embroidered slippers that went with the suit.

“Your sister. Were you in that wedding too? Because I’d love to see that picture. I imagine she’s every bit as gorgeous as you and your brother.”

He sighed. “She is. I wasn’t in the wedding. She married a white guy and he was very traditional. Meaning her out gay brother was not going to be in the party.” That wasn’t all, but he would just as soon not remember everything. Not wanting to wasn’t super effective. It was one of those things that crawled out from under a mental rock every time he got anxious. “I should tell you this. Can I tell you this? It’s stupid and enraging, I shouldn’t.”

"Tell me." She patted the silk suit one more time and then went to sit cross-legged on his bed. He sat beside her, one knee tucked up and the other foot on the floor. Karen made a 'please proceed' face and took his hand.

Willem said, "They got married three years ago. I went back a year later for a festival. Our parents had this party in the backyard, a big buffet cookout kind of deal. Stephanie's husband made a pass at me."

"What?!"

"Right? I'm standing at the buffet table and he comes up behind me and stands really close. You know, hip right up against my ass." Karen made a disgusted sound that said she was familiar with this maneuver. "And he says, want to get together later. He was a little bit drunk. I was like, you motherfucker. I turned around to push him back. Not with my hand where it would be obvious. With my shoulder, and my elbow in his ribs, because I didn't want to make a scene."

"I've done that exact same thing."

"I hate that we have to know how to do that. Anyway, I said, all pleasant and smiling, if I thought you would make my little sister cry, if I thought you would ever hurt her, I would put this satay skewer through your eye right now. Do I need to do that? And he blinked. Seemed to realize I'm taller than he is. Did this kind of fish thing with his mouth, and then said no. I didn't say anything else, only watched him while he went over to Steph. He was a little subdued but he seemed to be making nice. So I found a corner to hide in until the shakes went away, but Laurence found me. My brother. He said, what happened. And I told him, and he believed me. A while later I saw him talking to Steph and her husband. Stephanie looked really upset, and I could see she was asking him if it was true. I could tell he wanted to lie. But he looked over at me and I don't know what he saw but he, like, sagged. I left not long after that. Got in my rental car, drove into Chicago, went to a club and picked somebody up. Went back to Mom and Dad's house the next day. I don't think they know anything ever happened."

"Oh my God, that absolute asshole. What did your sister do?"

"They're still married. They started seeing a counselor. She told him, being bi is not what bothers me. It's the hitting on my own brother at my parents' house. It's the potential for cheating. Apparently he said something about this only happens when I'm drinking, so he's in AA. Laurence laid down some rules. Nobody fucks with Laurence. He's two years younger than me and he's up for partnership at his law firm. He'll be a senator by the time he's forty, I'll bet." Willem tried to sound as if he felt unconflicted pride.

"He looks sweet." For some reason that made them both laugh. "But then, so do you."

Willem shook his head. "I am not sweet. There's a lot wrong with me." Karen made an annoyed sound conveying disagreement, which made him love her more. "I've been working on myself a long time. Anyway, whatever. That suit? You think so?"

"If it was, like, turquoise or hot pink maybe no," she said. "But it's subtle. Dressy and elegant but not too formal. Your guy is going to love it."

"Is he my guy?" Willem tried to make a joke of it.

Karen gazed at him affectionately. "Do you want him to be?"

Willem blinked. Swallowed. Nodded. She patted his knee. Leaned over to kiss his cheek. Stood up to go. "Thank you," he said.

"See if you can get a picture of the two of you together," she said. "Because I'm totally dying of curiosity."

And he said he'd do his best, because he wanted to see the two of them together more than he could even believe.

Chapter 11

Richard sent a text when he pulled up outside Willem's house. Got out of the car, because it seemed important to be on his feet for this. He didn't have to wait long. Willem came out through the front door, laughing over his shoulder. Then he turned, saw Richard, and blinked. "You would think we planned this."

"That is gorgeous," Richard said. *You are gorgeous*. "It does look as though we planned this." The two jackets were fabulous together. With Willem in those fairytale-kingdom slippers and Richard in his boots, they were very close in height. Richard hoped someone would get a good picture. He opened the passenger door. Willem started to get in, then lifted a hand. Lightly brushed the backs of his fingers up Richard's cheekbone and into his hair. It felt like a kiss. Then he smiled, a little uncertainly, and got in the car.

It was a forty-minute drive across town to the church in Inglewood. They made occasional, slightly awkward conversation on the way. There was a valet service at the venue, which only made sense. Richard turned his car over and they walked through the mob of festively-dressed people milling around outside, separated from a row of paparazzi by a team of security people. He spotted Rory and Dana, took Willem's hand, and led him that way. Made the re-introduction and said, "Tell us what Dexter was like to work with on your show. Willem's a friend from his dance days."

"I figured," Rory said, giving Willem an unconvinced look. Dana elbowed her and started telling on-the-set stories that soon had others gathered around.

Richard gave Willem a sideways glance and collected a grateful look in return.

When Richard loosened his grip Willem instantly let go of his hand, and immediately felt bereft. But the group was easy. Everyone was in the mood to have a good time. After a while Dana seemed to throw the storytelling ball to him. So he came up with an anecdote about working with Dexter – and pretty much every other dance extra in California – on a big-budget movie musical a few years back. As soon as he wrapped that up there was movement toward and into the church.

There was no 'bride's side' or 'groom's side.' The usher took them to the first available seats. The church was decorated simply, with an array of fluffy-looking baby Norfolk pines and white poinsettias. Willem wanted to hold Richard's hand again, told himself he was out of his mind, and tried not to fidget. It felt like ages before the procession started. That didn't take long, because it was a small wedding. A best man came down the aisle in a Black Watch plaid jacket. Dexter followed in a white dinner jacket, looking like a legit movie star. Then came the maid of honor, in a Black Watch pencil skirt with a snug black velvet top and a fantastic vintage-looking green rhinestone necklace. Richard and Willem glanced at each other and smiled because she was so pretty. Finally the bride walked down the aisle, wearing a perfectly-fitted 1960s-style pencil dress in a shimmering gold and silver plaid. Every woman in the church (and quite a few men, including Richard and Willem) made appreciative sounds.

It was the traditional ceremony, with a lot of great music. After the first song, Willem was all in. He didn't forget about his date, but he could relax, stop worrying about that situation, and start enjoying what was happening for Dexter and Rita. A breakthrough role, then a movie, and now this. They looked so blazingly happy when they walked down the aisle together.

And they'd done everyone a huge favor by booking their reception not at some posh beach hotel, but right there in the church's fellowship hall. It was done up Hollywood style, though; the ceiling was draped with white tulle and lit with string lights. The walls were covered with giant black and white photos, glamour shots of great movie stars, framed with silk flowers in gold, silver, and white. They had a lavish buffet, endless champagne, professional servers, and live music from a local R&B band. Willem led the way this time, taking Richard's hand and bringing him over to congratulate the bride and groom. "Dexter, Rita, so happy for you." Hugs and kisses were exchanged. "This is my friend Richard Hollister." Introductions, handshakes, and a brief volley of how-do-you-know. Then Willem asked, "Are you doing a wedding dance?"

Rita snorted. Dexter rolled his eyes and said, "She said no. We're going to sing a little something instead."

"Oh, fantastic! Can't wait! Richard, Dexter can really sing. You're in for a treat." Willem raised his eyebrows at Rita.

She said, "Trust me, a song is a much better option than a dance from me."

"Word," someone said. They all turned to look; it was the maid of honor. "Hi, I'm Dolores the hair wizard. Doesn't she look gorgeous? That's because of me."

"Girl, please." Rita was trying for Disapproving Face, but she was too happy. "If you don't watch out I'm gonna chuck this bouquet right at you."

She did, in fact, seem to be aiming the bouquet at Dolores. The hair wizard neatly deflected and the flowers landed in the hands of a statuesque Filipina, producing a chorus of "Oh!" Everybody seemed to be looking for someone, who turned out to be a tall Middle Eastern man making an 'I'm trying!' face. Then it was time for the wedding couple to sing. The R&B band backed them up for 'You Are The Best Thing,' and they sounded great. Half of the guests were taking video with their phones. Richard and Willem glanced at each other, then away. It was as if they wanted that song to be about them, but couldn't be sure it was.

Richard stopped at one glass of champagne, since he was driving. He noticed that Willem stuck to sparkling water again. It might have been for health reasons, but Richard was putting things together. If what he suspected was true, he and Willem had more in common than he'd thought. Except of course Willem didn't know about the anorexia. Richard was hiding it better these days.

It was never not a thing. He always had to be aware of potential triggers, always had to work at minimizing the obviousness of his coping mechanisms. He hadn't done so well this evening. The tendency toward chaos in a buffet environment worked against him. But nobody noticed, because – even more than usual – he wasn't the center of attention.

Except from Willem, whose attention grew more intense as the evening progressed. It was because this was a wedding, Richard told himself. An emotional event, and everyone around them seemed to be in love. Well, except for Dolores.

Willem was relieved when the servers moved all the tables back to open up the floor for dancing. He didn't even ask, simply wrapped an arm around Richard and took him to the center of the room. Barely aware that the first song the band played was 'Take It To The Limit.' He knew enough waltz to make it work, and Richard followed perfectly. "You're so good," he said when the song ended. "I'll bet you lead that well, too."

"Want to find out?" Richard was smiling.

"I don't know how well I'll follow. I don't have a lot of experience." It felt like they were talking about something other than dancing.

"Do you trust me?" It sounded like a serious question.

For a second Willem wasn't sure he did. Wasn't sure he could. He saw his own uncertainty reflected on Richard's face. "That's not a question we should ask each other yet, is it?"

"Maybe not." Richard wasn't smiling now. "Never mind. I'll follow."

Willem felt sick. "I'm sorry. No. We have to start somewhere. I have to start." He tuned in to the music, country blues. A slow dance. "Will you dance with me?" Richard nodded. He moved in as if expecting Willem to lead again. But Willem put his left hand up on Richard's shoulder, offering his right. Richard glanced up quickly, startled. Then, still making eye contact, he slid his right arm around Willem and stepped into the dance.

A little over an hour later, people were beginning to make going-away motions. Willem and Richard finally stopped dancing and left the floor. They went to find Dexter and Rita for one more round of hugs and kisses, then swung by the restrooms. Eventually they joined the queue of departing guests, waiting for the valet service to bring their cars. "Thank you for asking me to this," Richard said, because he had to say something. Standing there in silence was too uncomfortable. "I had a good time."

Willem didn't know if he was really hearing a note of finality, or if he was only afraid of it. "I did too. Thanks for coming with me." After a moment he added, almost out of desperation, "Those boots are great."

"As soon as I tried them on I thought, why didn't I think of this before." Richard glanced at his date. Willem did not have the face that went with 'thank God this is almost over.' He was close to smiling, though clearly somewhat anxious. "You remember Sam and Mateo. Sam runs a tux shop and he's really good at the fashion thing. He hooked me up last year." With that, miraculously, they were talking. About clothes, about dancing, about anything and everything, all the way back across town. When Richard pulled up at Willem's house he was still laughing over a cruise-ship story. He put the car in park, but left the engine running. He didn't want the night to be over. It needed to be, for a lot of reasons. "Can I call you?"

"I was about to ask that." They smiled at each other. "Can I kiss you? I missed kissing you." He shouldn't have said that.

But Richard said, "God, yes," and leaned over. Willem met him halfway, one hand going to his face and then into his hair. He made some kind of sound when Richard's mouth opened. It was the kiss he'd wanted since closing night. He completely lost track of time. What seemed like hours later, they parted. Stared at each other. Said, "I'll call you," almost in unison. Willem touched Richard's mouth, as if he couldn't help himself. Then smiled, opened the door, and got out of the car.

Richard was slightly shaky when he got home. Part of it, he knew, was reaction to that kiss. That wonderful, tantalizing, intoxicating kiss. The rest of it was hunger. He worked out how much he'd had to eat that day, worked out the bare minimum he needed to keep on track, consulted his refrigerator, and began. An apple, washed and dried and cut carefully into eight segments. Dill Havarti cheese, four slices, each bisected into nearly-identical bites. A hard-boiled egg, quartered. All neatly arranged on a plate and taken to his little table with a glass of water. A bite of egg first, with a dash of salt. Then apple, then cheese. A couple of ounces of water to drink. Apple and cheese again. More water, then repeat. Each time, he arranged the remaining food so that no gaps were apparent, so his disorder couldn't tell him 'you've had this much, that's enough' with sufficient authority to derail him. Sitting there under his dimmed brass chandelier, still dressed, thinking of nothing but what he was eating. The more consciously he could do this, the more effective it was. Awareness of the flavors and the textures, the contrast. Appreciation as he felt his body respond to nourishment. Each bite a victory.

There were times he was able to eat more, but the volume he could manage at any given sitting was small. He'd been asked once, on a date, if he'd had gastric bypass surgery. After a moment to wonder if that was really the most obvious thing, he said it was a medical condition, but not that one. Then he changed the subject. It was easy to do when someone wanted to get him in bed. The thought made him remember Willem's kiss again.

For a moment, after that first dance, he thought they were on the edge of trouble. Maybe even disaster. It was a tricky situation, because it seemed neither of them had said what they wanted to say sixteen months ago. He hadn't dealt well with Willem leaving. Willem – that good-looking guy on the cruise ship notwithstanding – apparently hadn't dealt well with Richard walking away. He knew how easy it was to mask pain with sex. He'd done it for years himself.

But it was a work night, and he couldn't sit here thinking about that. He cleaned up the kitchen, undressed, stood for a minute in front of the full-length mirror on his closet door, and wondered if they had a chance. Willem liked this body once. It was in better shape now, stronger, thanks to all the dancing with Rory and the others. It would never be a spectacular body like Willem's, but it was (as he'd told Dr. Simon) functional. He touched himself, imagining it was Willem's hand, and watched the result. Then he lay down on the bed and closed his eyes, because that way he could see Willem while he felt this. He could remember how it felt to follow, and to lead, and to kiss. He could imagine Willem's mouth on him as it had been before, so long ago, it had been so long, he wanted that again. He bucked up into his hand and let the climax come. Eyes still closed, breath slowing, wondering if Willem did this too.

The first thing Willem did after shutting himself in his room was carefully disrobe. He hung the silk suit from the curtain rod to let it air. The rest of his clothes lay on the floor where they'd fallen while he leaned against the wall and jerked off. "Jesus," he said out loud a few minutes later. That kiss. Even better than he'd remembered, or imagined, or hoped. There was something about Richard's fine sharp bones under his hand, and the feel of his hair. Thick and wavy, robust as the rest of him didn't seem to be, though there was considerable strength in that wiry body. Willem palmed the head of his cock, went through into the bathroom to wash his hands, and wondered what to do now.

He wanted Richard. Wanted him again, or still, and there was more to it than simple physical desire. But it was so unfamiliar, and they had that history. That not-so-promising beginning, though he supposed the only real problem was the way they'd left it. If he had said, 'I want to see you when I come back, and I will come back,' maybe Richard wouldn't have left that way. If Richard had said, 'I want to see you when you come back,' maybe Willem would have been able to resist Jesse.

He didn't want to make the first move again. If he did, he was always going to wonder. The wedding tonight – in fact, the whole of the past eighteen months, now that he was thinking about it – made it hard not to circle back to the conviction that there really was something wrong with him, or about him, beyond what he already knew. Why hadn't he ever tried to have a real relationship before? Why had it always seemed like something that could wait, something less important than the next gig? Now here he was at thirty-five, alone, essentially putting the cap on the career he'd worked so hard for, because he was never going to be a star, and patching together a living that amounted to nothing. He was starting to hyperventilate. "Stop it," he told himself, again out loud. It was the same familiar mental loop, one that used to send him straight to alcohol. He finished washing up, went to bed, and lay awake a long time. He had to do better, and he had to start now.

He didn't sleep well. Knew he looked tired when he got to Tidal Flow. Led his first two classes as usual, then saw one of his private clients. After that he went to find the manager in the tiny office tucked behind the almost-as-tiny reception area. He tapped on the half-open door. "Hi Rhonda. Do you have a minute?"

"Hi Willem, sure. Come in. What's on your mind?"

He closed the door behind him. "I talked to Kevin the other day and he said he's cutting back so he and Paul can travel. I want his hours." He said that fast. "I need to know if there's such a thing as a full-time job here."

Rhonda sat back, eyebrows up. She was the sole full-time employee of the studio, which was incorporated only because of the high potential liability. "I wasn't sure you were that committed to this career."

He tried not to react to that. In his world, always showing up meant committed. Getting and keeping the certifications, the personal liability insurance, managing the records, doing his own billing and bookkeeping: it was all wearing him out, but he didn't let anything slide. If that wasn't 'committed' he honestly couldn't imagine what was. "I designed my class. It's full. I've hardly missed an hour since I started here. I don't have a rich husband or a trust fund." Those were low blows, but the truth was that Kevin and Karen both had a security blanket. He didn't. "I want to have a life. I need to stabilize. I can't do that when I'm split five ways." He took a breath, aware his voice was rising, and consciously de-escalated. "I'm sorry. I went to a wedding this weekend. I want the next one to be mine, so I need to figure this out."

Rhonda was diverted. "Oh, I didn't know you were in a relationship."

"I'm not." It came out a little sharp. "Yet."

"I can't offer benefits." It sounded like she was stalling.

"I have my own insurance." It made sense to keep his SAG membership. He didn't expect to get cast any more frequently than he had in the past, and he was definitely not going out for extra gigs anymore. But it was hard enough getting into the union, and getting an agent. Now that he had those things it would be idiotic to drop them. He didn't need benefits, as long as the average hourly rate didn't go down.

"Do you really want to teach eight hours a day?" Still stalling.

"I'm *already* teaching eight hours a day, it's just spread out over twelve hours." That sounded sharp, too. Sometimes it was more than twelve hours. "Can we talk about this seriously, or should I be talking to somebody else?" He didn't actually know if there was a better situation out there, unless he went fully self-employed. The clients he saw outside the studio paid more. The thought came as a surprise. What if he did go solo? He was already doing all that paperwork. What if he put some more videos online, training videos, and used those to attract new private clients? The group classes here were only ever going to pull people who already came to the studio.

Rhonda still hadn't said anything so he opened the door. "Think about it," he said, and went out. If she'd said, oh my God yes I was hoping you'd want to go full time, he wouldn't have even had that revelation. Her apparent resistance must have lit some kind of spark. He was still willing to make a deal. It didn't have to be forever. For now, he had half an hour before he had another session, and he was hungry. But he spent a few minutes on a text to Mandy, the owner of the ballet studio: *Would you have any interest in a class called yoga for dancers? May be looking to move from current location*

He spent most of his spare time over the next two days making a business plan. Mandy was texting constantly, and he threw the problem to her. She sent back two names that surprised him: Dmitri Vasko and Patrick Sarkisian. The owner of Shall We Dance and his husband, who happened to be one of the top tax accountants in Los Angeles. She left him a voicemail saying "Patrick knows business plans and Dmitri knows how to build a referral-based service business, one that's a luxury like ours. They'll help you. Good luck!"

Over those two days Rhonda didn't try to talk to him. Willem thought that was answer enough. He asked Karen if she would drop him off at CarMax on the following Sunday. He was going to need four wheels.

Chapter 12

Richard knew he had to call first. He wanted to have a reason that went beyond 'I want to kiss you again' and wasn't sure what it should be. An invitation to the Cabaret's December show was a possibility. On the Wednesday after the wedding, he was over at Rory and Dana's having a dinner meeting. They had all the other Cabaret principals on Zoom, working out the 2018 schedule. Once that was done and everyone else was off the line, Rory said, "Okay, so, Willem."

Richard didn't ask what she meant. "Thank you for that picture." She'd texted him one, the morning after the wedding. If they hadn't shared that kiss he would have had to delete it immediately. Since they had, he probably never would. "We left it at 'I'll call you,' and it's my turn. I need to have some activity planned but I don't know what."

"Do a dance," Dana suggested. "We saw you at the wedding."

"That was social dancing!"

"Give me a break." Rory topped up their wineglasses. "He's a professional. You're the next best thing to a professional. Had you ever danced together before?" She could see the answer was 'no.' "Then what do you have to lose? It's a great way to find out if you can get along out of bed." He sputtered with laughter. Rory waited, more or less patiently, then added, "I'll bet he misses it. I missed the fuck out of it."

Dana reached over a dog to pat her wife's leg. "Thank God for naggy friends."

Richard stifled another laugh. "You don't mean for the Cabaret, do you? Oh crap, you do."

Rory gave him a look. "We just spent half an hour bitching about all the people who aren't available in January. We need bodies. Why Elena had to go and get pregnant again I will never know. Those lazy-asses Sam and Mateo were like, well hey, let's go on vacation! Vince and Michelle are out because of their competition schedule. If Hiro asks Anya one more time she's going to shank him. Dmitri and Patrick are going to Argentina in a minute and who knows when they'll be back, or if the boss will have time to put anything together with anyone."

They'd already been through all this. Richard was amused and touched by the transparently over-explainy detail. "We always have plenty of submissions from outside Shall We Dance. But okay. I'll ask him. God knows I'd love to dance with him. And he doesn't hate country music."

"I noticed," Dana said dryly. "Do it now so we know you didn't chicken out."

"Hey." He tried to look offended. It probably didn't come across. He picked up his phone and composed a text. Before he sent it, he showed it to both women for approval: *Hi Willem. Loved dancing with you Sunday. Here with the team talking about Mating Dance. Would you be interested in working up a routine with me for January? If not, maybe I could take you to dinner sometime soon.* He added a smiley face and sent it off. "There. You can't say I didn't try."

They seemed to be satisfied. Rory said, "I'll post the schedule. Let us know what happens. Give me back my cat." Richard hoisted Spike off his lap and onto hers. The cat hissed half-heartedly at the little dogs on either side of her. "Spike, for God's sake, they're *your* dogs."

Dana walked out of the den with Richard. "Everything's okay?"

“Seems to be,” he said. “Thanks again for all your help.” He kissed her cheek. “You and the cherubim.”

“And the cat. Drive safe.”

Willem was putting the finishing touches on his draft business plan when he heard his text notification go off. Halfway assuming it was Mandy again, he didn’t pick up the phone right away. Instead he proofread the document once more, proofread his cover email to Patrick Sarkisian one more time, then mentally crossed his fingers and sent it off. The worst that could happen was that Patrick would come back with a long list of things he’d forgotten, or that he hadn’t known should be included. Internet research got him to this point; now he needed an expert consultant.

And also to see what the ballet girl had to say. He woke up his phone and said “Oh!” Read the text from Richard, smiling, surprised but delighted. Even if they didn’t get cast for the show, it would be so much fun to make a dance. Of course, with Richard as the show runner, they’d have to really suck for it not to pass the audition. He turned back to his laptop and went to the Underground Cabaret website to check out the theme. Maybe the other man already had something in mind for ‘Western Stars.’ He sent a text: *Hi Richard I’d love to work on a dance with you. Do you have music? When and where to start? Also dinner would be great. I’m going to buy a car on Sunday. Maybe after that?* He sent it off before he could convince himself that was too much.

A reply came back promptly: *Where are you going car-shopping? Want some company?*

Did he ever. *CarMax in the South Bay and yes. Karen was going to drop me off*

I'll take you. That way if they don't have something you want you won't be stranded. What time should I come for you?

He couldn't write 'now,' especially since 'come for you' took him to a very non-car-related mental image. *Two o'clock?*

I'll be there. We'll talk about dancing

See you then. Willem added a smiley face and sent it off. He'd been so hoping Richard would call, and this was so much better than just a call. A whole afternoon and evening together again. Doing grown-up things again. And now he had the new business idea to talk about, too. It was looking like a very eventful week. He was excited; it felt like he was in a completely different place from Sunday night.

Richard got back to him the next day with a track, 'Trail of Broken Hearts' by k.d. lang, and a note that said only *rumba?* Willem listened to the track, thought *huh*, and listened to it again. It was a pretty song, but the lyrics definitely raised a question. Maybe they could talk about it Sunday, or the next time. Whenever it was that they could start digging into it, because what Willem knew about rumba didn't go far beyond what he'd done with Richard – or rather, what Richard had done with him – at the wedding. He knew the guy was a qualified instructor, but he was hoping to bring a bit of theater arts into the project. *Don't get ahead of yourself.* This was enough. This was not something a man would suggest if he didn't want to spend some serious time together. And it wouldn't have come with a dinner invitation if the man in question wanted to keep it strictly business.

The next three days seemed to take a month to pass.

Richard knew he was taking a chance with that track. Some music didn't mean anything, some had subtext, and some was obvious. This was definitely on the obvious side. But he and Willem had done a little too well at not saying things, and Richard didn't want to risk that again. Having Willem basically say 'I need to learn to trust' was major. As soon as they started working on the dance, all kinds of things were likely to come out. Things that Richard didn't say, maybe *couldn't* say, before. And maybe before was the wrong time anyway. He'd done some good work in the past sixteen months. Come a long way. He so hoped he and Willem were heading in the same direction now.

He texted, as before, when he got to Willem's house. This time Willem came out to the car from the back. He was wearing jeans, a white button-down shirt, and a blazer. Slightly formal for a Sunday afternoon, but probably a good choice for a car-buying mission. And the blazer was a pastel plaid that made Richard smile. "Where did you get that jacket?" he asked when Willem got in the car. "I love it."

"Karen saw it at a thrift shop and thought I had to have it. God knows how she knew it would fit." He wanted to lean over and kiss Richard, who looked neatly casual in jeans, a knit shirt, and a cotton cardigan. He was fairly certain that wish was obvious. *Let's figure out where we're going first*, he reminded himself. "I'm so nervous. Thanks for this."

"My pleasure. What's the address?" Willem gave it to him. Richard entered it in his navigator. Then he backed out of the driveway and headed for the 405. He was fairly sure Willem noticed the snug fit of his shirt. It probably wasn't fair to wear something like that, something intentionally body-conscious. But he was going to suggest swinging by Shall We Dance before taking Willem home, if they weren't in two cars by that time, and maybe if they were. It would be good to take a crack at the dance as soon as possible. Willem hadn't commented on the music, which Richard took to mean he was okay with it, but 'soon' was the time to find out if he was right. "So what made you decide now was the time to get a car?"

"Well, it looks like I'm going solo." Richard made an interested sound, so Willem told the whole story, starting from first going to Mandy's studio with Karen. "And I didn't ask how she knows Dmitri and Patrick, or what she told them, but I know they were on their way out the door for this trip and they still took the time to give me so much great advice. I remembered Dmitri, from last year, being the guy who barely spoke. But he wrote me this terrific letter. I will never delete that."

"He's wonderful," Richard said. "I landed in that studio by accident and it changed my life." Possibly saved it, but he wouldn't go there yet. "So what kind of car do you have in mind?" That discussion got them most of the way to their destination. Once they arrived, Richard was pleased (and, honestly, a little surprised) to find Willem focused, assertive, and decisive. When he examined the surprise, he realized that he had no idea what it took to actually succeed, over the long term, as an entertainer. He'd quit before he had to do it himself. Until then, his mother handled everything. Maybe they could talk about it sometime, after Richard told him everything. If he could.

They test-drove three different vehicles. Willem knew which one of the three he wanted, and the price was acceptable. He didn't even hate the color. Richard watched and listened as the transaction progressed. The salesman clearly assumed that they were a couple. At first he was kind of jokey about it, but after ninety minutes of Richard's mostly-silent attention and Willem's 'no bullshit please' attitude he was all business. It wasn't that long since Richard bought his car. He'd gone alone, and remembered how hard it was to keep track of all the details.

Willem was impressively prepared. Two and a half hours after arriving, he signed the last piece of paperwork and got the keys to his almost-new Honda CRV. "Can you give me another half hour?" he asked Richard. "I want to call and update my insurance policy."

"Sure, no problem." Impressed all over again, Richard went to find them a couple of bottles of water. When he returned, Willem was talking to someone.

It was not quite six o'clock when he disconnected with a sigh. "Jesus, what a marathon. What a rock star you are. Thank you."

Richard smiled. "I didn't do much."

"You were here." Willem thought that was enough. "And I'm frickin' *starving*. Where should we eat? I have no idea what's down here."

"Me either. Let's find someone friendly and ask." The friendly person wasn't all that helpful, though. It sounded like getting to the place she recommended would take as long as getting to WeHo, and then they'd still be in the South Bay. So Richard counteroffered with the Italian restaurant down the block from Shall We Dance. "I was thinking maybe we could drop in to the studio and fool around with that track for a while, if it didn't get too late."

Willem didn't even try to hide his delight at this suggestion. "Awesome. Perfect. I was hoping we could work on it soon. Will there be a lot of people there?"

"I'll be surprised if *anyone* is. There was another wedding today. Everyone who would have been rehearsing for the Cabaret would be at this thing."

"But not you?" Willem would have thought Richard would be included in anything studio-related.

"No, these people aren't personal friends of mine. Andy Martin and Victor Garcia."

"Oh shit! Really?! They got married? Jesus, it took them long enough." Richard laughed. Willem was grinning. "Okay. Let's get on the road. We can park at the studio? Great. See you there." Again he wanted to kiss Richard; again he figured the other man knew that; and again he resisted. Instead they exchanged smiles and went to their cars.

By the time they were seated, Willem was ravenous. It wasn't until they were halfway through dinner that he sort-of-noticed the way Richard was eating. He remembered this from before. Hadn't been aware of noticing it then, because at the time he was focused on getting the guy into bed. It wasn't weird, exactly. Oddly methodical, slightly ritualistic, unusually … attentive. He wasn't going to ask about it. There wasn't anything off-putting about it. It was simply another unique thing about Richard. That chicken marsala looked almost as good as the lasagna Willem was mowing through, and it smelled phenomenal. "Could I try a bite of that?"

"Sure." Richard didn't give him one of the already-cut bites. Instead he cut a new one, and lifted the fork as if to feed it to Willem. *Oh really*, he thought, and smiled as he opened his mouth. He made a production out of taking the chicken off the fork. Richard's pupils dilated. He put the fork back in his own mouth for a second before setting it on the rim of his plate and lifting his wineglass. "You're so sexy," he said, eyes on Willem.

"You are. We should talk about that."

"We will."

Richard put his leftovers in the fridge at the dance studio. As predicted, the place was deserted; he'd had to use his key to let them in. That suited him fine. He had a feeling they needed to say a few things fairly soon, because it was clear they were both still interested. The physical attraction was, if anything, even stronger than it had been the year before. "I thought preparing a dance together would be a good way for us to learn some things about each other. To be honest, it wasn't my idea. Dana suggested it. Rory's wife."

"Dana Richardson. She's on 'Ten-31.'" He'd been aware of her during 'The Great Wave,' sharing stage-managing duties with Rory, but hadn't really spoken with her until Dexter's wedding.

"Right. I've known them a long time. Rory and I used to work together. She was in the records department at the law firm. She was my boss for a while. They're good friends."

"I want to ask what really happened last year. But maybe I shouldn't. We haven't even turned the music on." Richard nodded as if he agreed. He switched on the sound system, plugged in his phone, and retrieved the track. They both stood there in the dark room – the only lights Richard turned on were the ones in the corner with the kitchenette and sound system – and listened. Richard didn't say anything. When the music ended, Willem said, "Why this song? Because I had ideas but I don't know if they're right. My head's kind of spinning these days."

"I can imagine. Let's sit." Richard re-started the track, setting it to repeat. They went to a couple of the chairs lined up against the wall and sat down. Listened again, for half a minute. "It's because I could never stop looking back at you. I've always regretted walking away."

Willem's voice was soft. "Why did you?"

"Because I never felt like anyone wanted me to stay. Or that *they* wanted to stay. You weren't going to stay. So I left before you could."

Willem thought *fair enough* but was caught by something else. "Why wouldn't anyone want you? Why wouldn't *everyone* want you?"

That question went straight to Richard's heart. He blessed Willem for saying that. He couldn't begin to answer him. "Oh, honey, you don't want me to go into all that right now. We have work to do." He was hoping they could proceed. That they could start building something, so that when the rest of it started coming out – which it would, it had to, if this was going to work they needed to be able to tell each other everything – they would have a foundation.

Willem was leaning forward, elbows on his knees, staggeringly handsome in the oblique light. Gazing straight at Richard. "Okay. We'll come back to that. Show me some rumba." They both took off their shoes and top layers, and went out in the middle of the floor. Half an hour later, he said, "Now can I mess around with it a little?" Richard smiled. Barely ten minutes after that, Willem said, "Okay, I feel like I missed something. You already know how to do this. God, this is great. When did you study jazz?"

“Ballet, jazz and tap when I was a kid. Then nothing till ballroom. But for the past year I’ve been going to kind of a class with Rory.” Willem’s eyebrows went up, asking for more. Richard said, “She invited me after Julia asked me to start working on the Mating Dance shows. Rory meets up with those girls from ‘The Great Wave.’ Ann and Bonnie. Sometimes Sam and Mateo come. Sometimes Mike and Paula.”

“You’re doing jazz with Mike Borodin.” Willem couldn’t have been more surprised if Richard said ‘I’m doing ballet with Tiler Peck.’ “Hallelujah Rock Star Wuthering Heights Mike Borodin.”

Richard bit his lip. It did sound unlikely. “He’s a good teacher,” he offered. “They all are.”

“Mother fucker! Well, you’re in trouble now. I thought maybe we could squeeze in a little bit of theater arts, but no mercy.” Willem rubbed his hands together with slightly alarming glee. “I know it’s getting too late to do much more tonight. And there’s other stuff to talk about tonight, so let’s leave it here and then next time, whatever, all bets are off.” Richard couldn’t help smiling. “Now.” Willem closed the distance and took both his hands. “I need to say something. Let’s sit down.” They went to the wall and sat cross-legged on the floor, still holding hands. “I wasn’t leaving.” He stopped as he heard himself. He tried again. “I wasn’t leaving *you*.” Richard understood that, he could tell. But his expression was something like resignation. “It didn’t matter, did it. Same outcome.” Richard nodded. Willem sighed. “I’m sorry.”

“Don’t be sorry. That’s life. Things begin and … things end.”

Willem wanted to hug him. Wanted to ask if they could start again, start from Chrome and the wedding and that kiss. Or maybe they’d already started, because this whole thing was Richard's suggestion. He was the one to call first, after that kiss. Maybe he wanted to be in love, too. "Have you ever been in love?" It was much too personal a question, or it would have been without those weeks last year.

Richard didn't think it was too personal. "Oh, of course." He could tell Willem would rather he'd said no. "The first time, I was fourteen. I was completely head over heels. I would have done anything, followed him anywhere. I gave him everything." He knew Willem was going to flinch when he said the next thing. Even Dr. Simon had. "He was twenty-eight."

"Jesus!" Willem's flinch was a full-body gesture of revulsion, but his fingers tightened on Richard's. "That wasn't a relationship, that was rape."

"Yes. I'm aware." Tone and gaze were sharp. Then he sighed, and softened. "You have to understand he was the first person who wanted what I was becoming. It took a long time before I stopped falling for that. And then for a long time I didn't let myself fall for anything."

Willem wanted to ask 'how long,' because it sounded as though Richard was saying he might be able to let himself fall, and why would he even hint at that if he didn't mean 'with you.' But he didn't ask. There was something else he needed to know. He needed to know how long Richard had been fighting his way back from that awful beginning. How old, if not how deep, the scars were. "Can I ask how old you are?"

Richard's expression was something between surprise and apology. "I thought I told you. Before. I'm thirty-one." A small, pained sound escaped Willem. "I know. On the plus side, there's a good chance I'll still look this way fifteen years from now." The damage was done long ago, and at least the bone structure was good.

Willem couldn't stand it. "I hope I'm around to see it," he said recklessly. "I think you're beautiful." He tugged gently. Richard let himself be pulled close. Not for a kiss. Willem hoped that was a case of 'not yet,' but they still had things to say. He settled back against the wall with Richard in his arms, their legs intertwined. "I still want you. I never stopped wanting you. But I'm bad at this. I've never had a successful relationship and I'm not sure I've ever truly been in love. I'm shallow, and I have a history of walking away when things get tricky. I do not want to walk away from you." He could feel Richard's breath, slow and controlled. "I'm not good with words."

"Neither am I." A ghost of a smile in Richard's voice. "I really only started talking to people, oh, sixteen months ago." Willem huffed out a laugh. "I have a decent education and I've been in therapy a long time. But I've never been a success at this either. I don't know where to start."

"What if," Willem stalled for a second. "What if we start here? Making this dance? We'll learn a lot about each other. Maybe go out. If you want to. But maybe we keep it public. Maybe we don't go to bed." He was thinking out loud.

Richard stiffened. *Doesn't he actually want me?* He'd said so, but then, "Why?"

"Because this isn't only about sex," Willem said in a rush. "We did that, it was great, but I want more. I want to kiss you, a lot," Richard laughed silently, "but if I kiss you in private there's going to be sex, because I want you. So we only kiss in public."

Richard thought about this, letting himself relax into Willem. "For how long?"

Willem's mind was racing. "Three months. Three dances. If it's ever not working, we'll know. You can't hide that shit when you're trying to make something." A sound of assent from Richard. "We go out, we see friends, we talk. Maybe our friends could tell us if we're getting somewhere." They both almost laughed. "I don't know a lot of people who've made it work. But you do."

"Yes, I do." There was only one problem with Willem's proposition. Richard wanted a kiss, right now, even though they were private. He didn't want to end this momentous conversation without reinforcing what he'd felt – what apparently they'd both felt – since Dexter and Rita's wedding. He wanted something to carry him through to the next time they saw each other, whenever that happened to be. "You won't kiss me now?"

Oh fuck it, Willem thought, and went for it. They were so close that it took only the slightest change of position. Richard's mouth opened under his immediately. *Oh Jesus Christ.* He was suddenly flooded with memories of their encounters last year. Of Richard's naked body against his, and the way they'd moved with such ease, as if they'd been lovers for years. The uncertainties and the discoveries all resolved with telepathic speed. So attuned to each other that neither of them had said anything except 'more' and 'now' and 'yes.'

He was half out of his mind, but eventually realized that Richard was underneath him on the hard cold floor. "Shit, sorry," he said against a wave of autumn-colored hair, then rolled over. Richard settled against him with a murmur, face tucked into the curve of his neck. They were both breathing fast, both so completely aroused that it would have taken only a few touches to finish. They kept their hands to themselves, lying still until they both relaxed. "And that's why,"

Willem said after a few minutes. "My God." Richard laughed silently against him. Willem wanted to say so many things. Eventually he settled for, "Am I important to you?"

"More than I can say." The hoarse voice was uneven.

"When we finish the third routine, let's talk again." He felt Richard nod. They lay there quietly for another minute. Then Richard sat up, and Willem sat up, and they both went for their phones to check their calendars and make a date for the next rehearsal.

Once that was done, it was time to go. Neither of them wanted to. Richard still had his phone in his hand. "I was hoping someone would get a good picture last week. Rory sent me one." He pulled it up and turned the phone around so Willem could see. He didn't know when, exactly, she took it. There had been a lot of rumbas and country waltzes, and this moment could have been during any of them. They'd been looking directly at each other, and the expression on both faces said 'I wish he would kiss me.'

"Oh my Lord." Willem swallowed. "Would you send that to me?" Richard didn't answer, only sent the picture. Willem felt his phone vibrate as it landed. He wanted another kiss so much it hurt. "Thank you for that. Thank you for today." Even if this was all they ever had.

Richard might have read his mind. "Until next time."

Chapter 13

Six days later, they put their audition on tape and sent it in. It might not have come together so fast if the evening group classes at Shall We Dance weren't suspended in December. Or if Willem hadn't declined, with every appearance of regret, taking over a daily evening class at Tidal Flow for an instructor who was out of town for two weeks. "Rhonda had to take it," he told Richard on the phone, satisfaction coming through loud and clear. "She was so sure I would. In my head I'm going, if I were your employee I would have to. I'm an independent contractor, and that's not in my contract. Whoopsie."

Richard suppressed a laugh. "Did you tell her why?"

"Nope. She doesn't need to know if my evenings go to being some rich old lady's walker or working as an Uber driver or getting my balls waxed." Richard laughed out loud. "It's none of her damn business. She has no idea I'm about to make tracks." Willem had a website almost ready to launch, and a series of eight short training videos completed and queued to post. He was a little surprised by how much he'd gotten done, and how many people were willing to help him. "Maybe I should feel guilty."

"I don't think so. You gave her a chance to lock you down." Richard was smiling. He'd heard a lot about the business plan over the past week. "Next year is going to be big for you."

"My parents are like, who are you." Willem's tone conveyed a shrug. "I told them I realized if I put all my hustle into one thing I could save a lot of time and potentially make more money. I was saving my pennies all those years living like a student. It was always so I wouldn't go broke between gigs. Then when I decided I was ready to stop chasing the dream, I realized I had enough to actually invest in myself. It takes me a while to get off the starting line sometimes."

"But once you do, you move fast." Richard didn't try to mask his admiration. All the discipline and creativity Willem needed to succeed in the uncertain world of entertainment had served him well. "It's exciting to see." He changed the subject. "Rory got in touch to ask if we'd like to come over for dinner soon. She probably wants to interrogate you."

"Oh, shit. Do all your friends think I'm an asshole?"

"Not because of anything *I* said." That made Willem laugh. Richard wasn't quite sure they were at the 'do things with friends' stage, though. "What do you think?"

"Any time." It was great to be able to say that. Great to know that yes, he could take time to have friends, to do things with friends that went beyond a gym date or a class or a coffee after work. He knew there would be days when he would start to panic over wasted time. But the whole point was to have that time. He thought he should say that. "There may be times when it seems like I'm freaking out. It's because there's a part of me that says every minute should go into hustling. But I have enough time, and I want to do these things, so I'll get over it. Please don't ever think if I seem kind of weird that it's because of you."

Richard had to take a breath. "I wish I could hug you right now. Thanks for that. I'll get back to the girls and let you know when they want to see us. Really, any time?"

"Any time. Now I'm going to work on a script for the next video." Willem wanted to say more, but 'wish I could hug you' was a good place to leave it. "Talk to you soon."

"I'll send you a text when I hear back. Good night." Richard could have stayed on the phone all night. Instead he disconnected, and then texted Rory.

A few days later, Willem drove over to Richard's place to pick him up. "It's so bizarre being able to go wherever whenever," he said as he pulled away from the curb. "I keep catching myself about to call for a ride. So what have you been up to?"

"Aside from work, nothing much," Richard admitted. "Since we got our dance blocked I've been going to the studio to work on the systems. Elena and Tony are moving to Italy pretty soon. She kept the office in great shape but there's a lot she taught me that isn't written down. So I'm writing everything out, and she'll review and revise before she goes. Dmitri will need to get another person in there."

"He's lucky to have you. When's he coming back, anyway?"

"God knows. Patrick will keep him away as long as possible, I think." That led into a discussion of vacations, something neither man had much experience of, until they got to WeHo.

Dana opened the cottage door as Willem was parking. "Hi guys," she said as soon as they were out of the car. "Sorry about the pack. Come on, you squirrelly little dimwits." The cat and the dachshund went back in the cottage. The fluffy white Malti-Pom came to Richard's feet. He obediently picked her up. Dana shook her head. "She is such a manipulator. How do you like your wheels, Willem? I had a Honda for twenty years."

"So far I love it. The only problem is I keep forgetting I have it. Hi Rory, good to see you."

"Likewise," said the chef. "Goddammit, Spike, do you *want* to get stepped on? It's pot roast. Who wants wine?"

"Not for me, thanks," said Willem. "I'm driving." Rory poured three glasses without comment, sending them all to the dining den. A few minutes later she brought the Crock Pot back and placed it on the table, where bread and butter and salad already waited. "God that smells amazing." Willem inhaled audibly. "When my schedule normalizes I'm totally learning how to make that."

"I will happily share my recipe." They all served themselves. "So guys, after the Andy and Victor thing last weekend we thought, has Richard ever seen 'Chicago,' and we thought maybe not."

Richard was puzzled. He'd definitely seen it, both the movie and the stage show. "Is this some special – oh!"

"Right." Dana was smiling. "The one Andy and Willem were in."

"You have that?!" Willem was amazed. "I don't even have that!"

Rory frowned. "Why don't you have that?"

"Because there was like a two-minute window of opportunity to ask for a copy of the recording, and I had to split and missed it, and then the guy who made it left L.A. and nobody knew where he went, and the only person in the cast I really knew was Robbie, and pestering him about it would have been a dick move." Rory and Dana made 'oh okay' faces. Willem turned to

Richard. “Robbie Campbell played Billy Flynn. The whole thing was a benefit for him. He had cancer and his bills were out of control. And he died anyway, which sucks. He was a real trouper.”

“That’s what Andy said. They knew each other from way back,” Dana said. “That’s the only reason Andy agreed to do the show. And the only reason I have a copy is I made him ask for one for me because he swore it was going to be the last stage thing he did, which thank God was a lie.” Richard and Willem snickered.

Rory swallowed some wine and went off on a tangent. “You should have seen their rings. These big Aztec-looking gold and emerald things. Like, straight out of an Indiana Jones movie.”

Dana nodded. “Victor said Andy found his – I mean Victor’s – in Mexico last year. Then they had one made for Andy. I’m so glad they finally tied the knot.”

“Was there some doubt?” Richard wouldn’t have thought so. Those two were notoriously inseparable.

“Not really but we were all afraid they would never make time for it. They don’t *stop*.” Dana sounded exasperated.

Willem glanced at Richard. “I was saying it’s going to take me a minute to get used to taking time for things. Things like this. Thank you for the invitation.”

“Our pleasure. Now tell us about that dance of yours. It’s the first submission we got, as Agent Smith knows perfectly well, and obviously we’re going to put it in the show. So talk.”

Willem and Richard took turns describing the way they’d worked out the choreography. Both women listened, paying as much attention to body language and tone as they did to the words. Richard caught Dana making a face at Rory that seemed to say 'this might work.' He hoped so.

After the table was cleared, Rory and Dana moved a carved wooden room divider on the other side of the doorway to reveal a big flatscreen. Dana got everyone coffee while Rory set up the DVD. "This is going to be such a time warp," Willem said. "Eleven years ago!"

"I haven't seen it for years myself." Rory sat down with the remote. "I remember thinking it should always be staged with an all-male cast, but then I have a thing for men." Dana snorted. "Well can you blame me? We know some amazing men."

"Yes we do," Dana allowed. "I guess it's better for me this way. God forbid you had a crush on Vicky or Sharon."

"Only for a minute," Rory said. Both men laughed. "I got over it. Anyway!" She pressed 'play' and they settled back to watch.

Willem said, "Heaven on earth, those legs," when Andy came on as Velma Kelly.

"Yours are that good," Richard said without thinking. Dana and Rory both giggled. He glanced at Willem, who was blushing a little. "At least they were last year."

"Hush!" The women were laughing out loud. Willem threw his arm around Richard's shoulders and pulled him close. Kissed his cheek and murmured, "Watch this thing." Richard relaxed against him, smiling.

"You were so cute," he said when they were in the car, heading back to his place. "You looked about sixteen."

"I was a pretty little chorus girl," Willem agreed. "God that was fun. I had the worst crush on Robbie. He was a legend. Being in that show with him is probably the highlight of my career, even though hardly anybody saw it."

"Career number one." Richard patted his thigh. "You're still young. Who knows what might happen in career number two. Maybe you'll be the next Bikram."

"Oh Jesus no. I hate hot yoga." They both snickered. After a minute Willem shot him a sideways glance. "This is going to be rough if you keep flirting with me."

"You said we could kiss in public," Richard pointed out. "I was kind of hoping that meant everything up to and including kissing."

Willem took a moment to admire that ingenious extrapolation, congratulated himself for stringing those words together, thought *this whole thing is making me smarter*, and said, "I cannot actually argue with that." He glanced over again; Richard was smiling at him. "God you're gorgeous. As soon as I stop this car you need to get out or all my good intentions are going straight to hell."

"Mine too." Richard thought Willem might be driving somewhat slowly as they approached his apartment. He didn't mind at all. He was in the absolute opposite of a hurry to be left alone at home instead of sitting in a quiet, private, intimate place with this man.

Dr. Simon stopped in the act of coming out from behind his desk to stare at his client. "Okay. What happened? This is not the Richard Hollister I saw last month."

Richard took his seat, waiting until his therapist was situated before saying, "He came back."

"The guy from last year?"

The tone was so astonished that Richard might have been insulted if he wasn't so close to laughing. Instead, he nodded. "He was at the Cabaret show before Thanksgiving. We ran into each other at the bar, and I apologized for walking out on him. Fixed it so he could stay for the after-party so we could talk. And then he asked me to go with him to a wedding."

"Okay, wait. Hold on. You haven't seen him for more than a year, you roll up on him at a bar –" Richard laughed. Dr. Simon continued, "And he asks you to a wedding? I'd say he's been thinking about you a lot. Now, do I need to ask what you said?"

"I said yes as soon as he stopped talking." Richard waited for the counselor to stop laughing. "The wedding was on Sunday the third. We danced. We talked. When I took him home, we kissed. And then the next Sunday, my God, it was like four dates in one."

"Tell me." Dr. Simon settled back, notepad and pen at the ready.

"He was going to buy a car. I offered to go with him. After that we went to dinner. Then we went to the dance studio for a while. I asked if he wanted to put together a routine with me, for a show."

"What." A hand actually up to stop him, tone loaded with surprise. "You suggested doing a show together. And he said yes?" The first thing was fairly astonishing, squarely in the 'breakthrough' category. The second was fireworks. It was so rare for a client to come in with a big piece of good news that he always took time to celebrate it.

Richard clearly agreed with that. He leaned forward, elbows on his knees, openly smiling. "My friends said I should. They said, it's a good way to see if you get along outside of bed. And I thought, you know, okay. Because we know we're good in bed. But maybe he wanted more than that, and asking me to a wedding made me think maybe he did."

Dr. Simon gazed at him over the top of his reading glasses for a minute. "Then what?"

"We worked on a dance, and we talked a lot about some important things. And we agreed that we want to try again." He waited to hear from the therapist. There was no comment for a minute as Dr. Simon made some notes. "He suggested we should stay out of bed for a while."

A big 'what the fuck' gesture made Richard laugh again. When he stopped, the counselor said, "You look way too happy for someone who's not getting laid."

"Well, the reason was if we stay out of bed we'll have to talk. We're going to date. We're going to meet each other's friends, and do things together like this dance. Three dances, actually. All that stuff I've been doing with my friends, he's impressed. He said, let's only kiss in public. And then he kissed me and I kind of had to agree that was probably a good idea." Dr. Simon snorted. "Anyway yes. I'm incredibly happy, and who knows what will happen, but the fact that he wants to try –" his voice broke. After a silent minute he said, "There's no way I could walk away again. It's not just that he's beautiful, and talented, and sexy. I learned so much about him in two Sundays out of bed. We finished the dance in a week. We've already had dinner with Rory and Dana."

"That's quite remarkable. Would you say you're trying something here that you haven't tried before?"

"Of course. You know that better than anyone. I'm terrified but I'm excited. I have not had someone come back to me before. I haven't had that person who said,

I think we might have something. And I know I'm not all that old, and maybe I haven't created the space for this kind of possibility before, and maybe what happened last year was necessary. Maybe I needed that shock. Realizing that I wanted something I couldn't have, but my neurosis was irrelevant. It wasn't anything about *me*, it was an unfixable situation."

Dr. Simon let that sit for a second. "Unfixable?"

"He was leaving. He might very well have chosen not to come back at all. But either way, in that moment, it was the end. For whatever reason, he decided not to let it be the end." Richard thought for another minute. "I realize that I needed that. Needed for someone to come to me with this notion that we could try. I've always been afraid to try. The thought of failure was so daunting. Even daily life is daunting. He said, this is about more than sex. He said, I want more, and he laid out a plan, and there was absolutely no reason for him to do that unless he's serious."

"And you didn't ask for anything."

"I didn't even *do* anything, except say yes."

"And you didn't hesitate. What went through your mind when you saw him again?"

"At the bar? I thought, thank God you're here. The first thing I did was apologize. And then we had no time to talk, so I hooked him up for the after-party."

"Did it occur to you he might not stay?"

"Oh yes. I kept looking for him, all through the second act. I kept thinking, my God, he's still here, maybe there's hope."

"What would you have done if he had, say, suggested going home together?"

"From the club?" Richard wanted to say he would have declined. "I'd like to say that I would have held back. But I missed him. But it was a work night. I might have made a counteroffer. I might have said, I can't tonight but how about this."

"In other words, you wouldn't have said no."

"I don't think I could have."

"That's interesting. Because if *he* asked *you*, that gives you the power. Would you say you felt compelled to say yes? To whatever?" Dr. Simon was wondering just how charismatic this other guy actually was. His client was not a weak man.

"Not compelled. Maybe driven. Because, you know, I was on the edge of tracking him down myself. I knew he'd come to some of the dance things. I knew he was changing his life in fairly serious ways. I couldn't help wondering if what happened between us was a motivation. The only reason I haven't talked about it before was I didn't want you to worry about me, always talking about something other than my thing."

"I knew you were dating," the therapist pointed out. "Contacting someone who I knew had, shall we say, positively impressed you would not be something I worried about." Richard stifled a laugh. "The past year has been a time of change for you, yes, but you have not been simply reactive. I'll be interested to hear how this develops. Meanwhile, how's your primary issue?"

"It kind of feels like not so much of an issue. I mean yes. Everything is business as usual. Conscious effort, every day, every meal. I've been thinking more about Willem than about my ridiculous disorder."

"Well, I'm glad you have something pleasant to think about. Don't let it distract you too much." This was the flip side of good news: the potential to forget that care must still be taken.

Dr. Simon was rarely that definite with suggestions, so Richard took it seriously. “I’ll be mindful,” he promised.

Chapter 14

There were fewer people than usual at the meeting. Either people were out of town for the holidays, or they were on a bender and would come crawling back in January. Willem had seen that happen a number of times; the holiday season was notoriously full of land mines. It was always a useful reminder of just how easy it was to fall off the path. Maybe with that in mind, when a moment came when nobody else was talking, he said, "Something's happened."

The leader said, "Can you talk about it?"

"I'm dying to talk about it." He smiled, so people would know it was a good thing. They were sitting in a circle, as they usually did. It was less challenging to start speaking, versus some meetings where the leader stood up at the front and the addicts sat in rows. Everyone could see you, and the leader was one of you. As, in fact, he or she always was.

He knew everyone here, their faces and stories if not their names. They all knew him. But he started at the beginning, as usual. "My name is Willem, and I'm an alcoholic. I have been sober for eight years and almost eleven months. I'll be thirty-six years old next month. I stopped drinking on my twenty-seventh birthday. Since then I have not been in a serious long-term relationship. Last year I met someone and had a serious short-term relationship that I didn't know was serious until it was over. It was over because I left town for a job, and for no other reason. This year I made some big changes in how I handle my working life, and a few weeks ago I met this person again, and we are trying again."

There was a murmur of pleased sounds. The leader said, “Congratulations. How did you meet?”

“We met both times because of dancing. He’s a ballroom dancer, and I was in musical theater.” There was the usual movement at ‘he’ from a couple of people who weren’t that comfortable with gay men being gay. Willem ignored it. This wasn’t the forum to deal with that. “I did a show last year that rehearsed at the studio where he trains. He teaches there now. This time I met him at Chrome. I was there to see a show, and he was running it. I saw him at intermission and we talked. I asked him to come with me to a wedding.” A couple of laughs, and several smiles. “Right? Hi, remember me, want to come to a wedding? Crazy. Didn’t even tell him whose it was, or where. But he said yes, so we went. And it was kind of weird because there were a lot of things we never said last time, and a lot of things I wanted to say, and a lot of things I was afraid to hear. But we danced, and eventually we talked, and it got easy enough that we both said I’ll call you.”

“And did you call him?”

“He called me. I was hoping he would, because I made the first move before, and you know what that’s like. Did he say yes because it was easy and he had nothing better to do.”

“Give me a break,” someone said. Willem turned to look at the speaker, a thirtysomething woman who hadn’t been coming to this meeting very long. “Oh come on. You know what you look like.”

“Irrelevant,” someone else said, someone Willem knew was a lawyer. “The fact that Willem is gorgeous probably makes it hard for him to know if someone is interested in him as a person. Same if he were rich.”

Willem nodded. “Thanks. Yeah, a little of that. It’s easy to find someone to, you know. But like I said, I haven't got a good history with relationships. So when he called me I was all, thank God. We've been talking a lot and I can't help feeling maybe this time it'll work. Maybe this time I'll get it right."

"And how is this affecting your sobriety?" The leader again, with an eye on the clock.

"It's a challenge, I won't lie. I always drank to shut down my brain, and now I have this other thing to worry about. What if I screw it up. What if he decides I'm not worth it. What if, what if, what if. When I'm with him I don't want to drink, even if we're in a place with alcohol. We go out to dinner, he has a glass of wine, and I'm fine. It's like, mine is not a situational addiction." A few people laughed. "And when I'm working, or with a friend, I don't want to drink. It's when I'm alone and the monkeys start banging on their drums. So it's a good thing I live where I live. I would have to go out to find a drink, and I always stop myself before I get to the door. Obviously I don't keep alcohol at home, and neither does my landlady."

"Is she an alcoholic too?" asked the lawyer.

"No, she's Muslim. Anyway, so far it's a good thing."

Various expressions of good wishes followed, and then the meeting broke up. Willem wasn't sure he was glad he spoke – he never was; it always felt like handing the world a knife and turning his back – but it was done. Some of those people were pulling for him, as he was for them. Next time they would ask how he was doing, and he would ask about them. That mutual investment in each other's success was half of the reason the program worked.

The next few weeks proceeded with what felt like an easy rhythm. Richard and Willem met up to practice their January dance, tossed around ideas for the next two shows, and only kissed in public. They went out to dinner with a variety of people, and to the Cabaret's December show, 'Tied Up In Tinsel.'

Willem's favorite number was from the Kung Fu Flyers. Richard preferred a mambo from four of the regulars. They fake-argued about it over a cocktail (for Richard) and a Pellegrino (for Willem) after the show. "It's getting late," Richard said after a glance at his watch. "I would invite you back to my place to discuss this some more if we weren't doing this whole chaste thing."

"Believe me, I have moments, like every day, when I ask myself why." Willem drank some of his sparkling water, watched Richard laugh, and wished he'd never made the suggestion. "But I can't help thinking we're talking more this way."

Richard thought *we could talk in bed*, and said, "Possibly." He drained his glass and took a breath. "Do you want to go out on New Year's Eve? I heard about this swing and salsa thing. I know it's not much advance notice."

New Year's Eve meant midnight which meant a kiss, and they both knew it. On the other hand, it would be in public, which was totally allowed. Willem didn't especially want to stay home alone, and he would really like to have something more meaningful to replace his memory of the previous December thirty-first. "Where?"

"It's at the Alexandria Ballrooms. And it's kind of pricey, but it would be my treat, because I got a raise." He'd been hanging onto that news for this exact type of scenario.

"Oh great! Good for you! But how pricey? If I see the details online am I going to feel like a gigolo?"

"I hope so." Richard swirled the ice cubes around in his glass and watched Willem laugh. They left not long after that, going up the stairs and out to the parking valet. They'd met up, because Chrome was out of the way to either of their places, and the going-home part of going places together was proving painfully tempting. Richard's car came up first. "I'll call you."

"I know you will." Willem leaned in for a kiss. "Let me know how we're getting to this thing on the thirty-first."

"I will." He had to get in the car. Had to go home alone again. Blew a kiss to Willem as he rolled slowly out of the parking lot, wondering if a month had ever in his life seemed so long. Wondering if he could possibly make it to the end of March without either dragging Willem into a bathroom stall somewhere, or spontaneously combusting. He wanted those hands, that mouth, that body more than he could ever have believed.

They made it through New Year's Eve (and a truly historic kiss), and then Richard had a proposition for Willem. The Sunday community classes at Shall We Dance, which were now on his roster of things to manage, had been a little disorganized in December. A friend of Dmitri's who used to teach two of the classes moved to Arizona with little notice. Richard dealt with it by calling for referrals from friends, continuing to cover Cardio Latin himself. But with Willem in this new business mode, he thought it was worth asking if he'd be interested in taking the other two classes. "Yoga and a thing we call Tone and Tune, which is basically calisthenics set to music. It's free, is the thing," he said over coffee. "It's pay what you can to the people who come, and the people teaching do it for love. And a little self-promotion."

"Which I could use." Willem sipped his coffee and thought about it. "You're always there?" He wondered if that would be too much. He didn't want Richard to get tired of him.

"Pretty much always." Richard hoped that was an inducement. Waited for Willem's next words. Then he couldn't wait. "I'd love to have a little extra time with you. I'd like to see you work."

Thank you. "I'm up for it, especially if you're usually here." The smile from Richard told him that was exactly the right thing to say. "Do you have to clear it with the boss?"

"He knows who you are. I'll tell him you're taking January, okay? And then if you like doing it we can talk about continuing."

"Same as our dancing?"

"Well." Richard lowered his gaze and took a beat, imagining this scene on stage, then added suggestively, "We'll be in public." He looked up from his coffee to see Willem grinning at him.

Richard was toward the side of the room as usual, half-watching Willem and half-watching the students, when the back door opened. Sam and Mateo walked in. They didn't see him at first. They saw Willem, and Mateo's eyes went wide. *Oh crap,* Richard thought guiltily. He'd managed not to tell them that Willem was back in his life, or rather the full extent of it. They were out of town or out of touch most of December, taking their delayed honeymoon, and then Mateo had been less present at the studio since he and Elena weren't going back out into competition. Richard hadn't been precisely avoiding his friends, but he also hadn't gone out of his way to arrange a rendezvous.

Sam wasn't displaying much of a reaction. They both took off their shoes, found space on the floor, and bent toward each other, saying something very low. "Hi guys," Willem said after cueing everyone out of the current pose. "Nice to see you." Then he cued the next thing. They went into it, but Mateo was looking around. After a few seconds he spotted Richard and made a 'what the fuck' face. Richard suppressed a laugh and did a 'tell you later' thing. He avoided Mateo's eye for the rest of the class because he didn't want to start laughing. Now that the moment had come, he couldn't wait to tell both his friends what had happened. What had so unexpectedly, gloriously happened.

During the short break between classes, there was a very brief moment when all four of them had a chance to stand close together and exchange a few semi-private words. "So," Mateo said, with a face eloquent of uncertainty. "Is this happening again?"

Richard said, "It's happening, but it's not quite the same thing, so I wouldn't say it's happening again." Mateo made a dubious sound. Richard smiled. "For the record, I think whatever it is, it's a good thing."

"That's enough for me," said Sam. "Nice to see you again, Willem. Are you leading the next one, too?"

"Yeah, I am. This is what I'm doing now."

"Tell us about it later." Sam patted his shoulder and wandered away to greet a couple of people.

Willem looked at Mateo. "I know I probably look like an asshole from where you're standing."

"No, you look like a total fox, the way you always did. Treat Richard right and we're fine." He also patted Willem before going to join Sam.

Richard was smiling at Willem. "I told you it would be okay."

Willem thought *I love you* and wished he could say it. "I'd better get this show on the road."

"I'll be in the office." Because they were in public, and because it was what they always did, and because they wanted to, they kissed. Then Richard went in the office and Willem got back to work.

Some of the regulars, and an instructor, showed up toward the end of Cardio Latin. That meant Richard was free as soon as he was done. After he wrapped up the class, he suggested brunch. He and Willem walked with Sam and Mateo a few blocks down the boulevard to a diner, waited a while for a table, talked about impersonal things. They were halfway through their meal before Willem said, "I'm so glad Richard had you when I went away."

"I almost didn't." Richard sipped coffee. "I wasn't good at reaching out. These guys made it easy. Rory, Elena, Julia … they were all right there waiting for me to look up and realize I didn't have to do it alone." He was hoping Willem would understand what he was getting at. *I love you*, he thought. *You're not alone.*

Willem glanced up, caught by a sense of subtext, and made eye contact. Read quite clearly 'I'm here for you, and they will be too.' He blinked and looked away, hiding his emotion. "I've always had friends on jobs," he said to the table. "My life has always revolved around the next gig. It'll be different now. I want you to know I'm serious," he said to the air in between Sam and Mateo. "I am not here to fuck him up."

Mateo nodded, accepting it. Sam said, "Then we're cool. I figured the only reason you'd be at Shall We Dance is if he wanted you to be. How do you like leading those classes?" And with that, the subject was changed.

By closing night of 'Western Stars,' Willem had left Tidal Flow, much to Rhonda's dismay, or so Karen said. He was working an average of fifty hours a week, spread out over six days. Sundays didn't feel like work, even though he was teaching those two free classes, because he was at least in the same room with Richard. Half the time Richard joined the yoga class, and Willem joined Cardio Latin. All the time, they went out for brunch afterward, with Rory and Dana, or Sam and Mateo, or – once, memorably – with Dmitri and Patrick. They also spent plenty of evening hours together, which kept him from feeling overworked. He even thought, sometimes, about organizing more work on the other nights, and had to tell himself not to be an idiot. He was doing fine financially, and keeping the freedom for spontaneity in his schedule had to be good for him. For them.

He hadn't yet decided when to take the next big financial step: getting his own place. He was starting to wonder if maybe he and Richard could live together. They hadn't discussed it, and until they took the next big relationship step he felt it would be premature. So he stayed in his safe little room and tried to believe that Richard meant it when he said he didn't care about that. Tried to believe everything that was going right was for real, and not some kind of illusion.

Their dance was definitely for real. They'd been working on it for so many weeks that neither of them had to think about it onstage. Willem couldn't remember a performance, or a connection, feeling so natural. It was almost scary, because it was new, and he didn't know if he could trust it. "I'm freaking out a little," he said out of nowhere, at the after-party. He and Richard were standing by the counter at the back of the downstairs lounge, watching other people dance. Richard had a glass of something and Willem had his trusty Pellegrino.

Richard set his glass down and leaned in close so they could talk easily. He slid one hand around Willem's back. "What's the matter, honey. Everything okay with work?"

"Yeah, everything's fine. More than fine. I could book full Sundays if I wanted to. And part of me wants to. It's like, I should strike while the iron is hot and book every available hour because it could all dry up tomorrow." He stopped talking, took a conscious breath, and felt Richard's mouth on his throat. He closed his eyes. *Oh God.* "And I want you so much, sometimes I think it's killing me."

"I want you too. I think about you all the time. It's almost worse because I remember how good we were together."

Willem turned a few degrees so they were standing front to front, touching from chest to thigh. He couldn't remember what he'd done with the bottle. One hand was in Richard's hair and the other on his ass. "And that was before I knew you. Jesus, Richard." They hadn't even kissed but they were both aroused. "It's too fucking bright in here." A soft laugh from Richard. The room was next-best-thing to dark.

"There are still things you should know. But they're things I don't want to talk about in public." Richard knew he needed to give up his last secrets before they made love again. He desperately didn't want to do it. "And they're things that might drive you away, and I can't stand the thought of that."

Willem couldn't imagine anything that would make him not want Richard. He said so. Then he looked around, remembered there was nothing like a clock in there, found Richard's hand and looked at his wristwatch. "There's another hour before we need to leave. Let's go back in the green room. It's technically public, but I think we'll be alone back there. And you know what, if we're not going to fuck tonight I need to jerk off right now."

Another soft laugh. Richard put a little space between them. "Every time I see you."

"Goddamn, sweetheart, don't tell me that." He took Richard's hand again and started for the stage steps.

Rory and Dana were sitting at a two-top on their way. "Heading backstage?" Rory saluted them with her wineglass. "Good. The sexual tension has been killing everybody."

Richard squeaked with horrified laughter. "Oh my God Rory." He couldn't tell her what they were (or weren't) going to do any more than he could tell her what he was about to say. Maybe she guessed, anyway. He would tell her everything the next time he saw her. He hoped whatever it was would be good news.

After verifying that the green room was empty, Willem pushed the couch in front of the unlockable door. Richard laughed again when he realized what was going on. "You really don't want anyone coming in here, do you?"

"I absolutely do want someone coming in here, and I want it to be me." The only question was whether he would do it here in the main room, or in the bathroom.

"Can I watch? Or can I help?" Both questions escaped him. He saw Willem flush, watched his lips part. Felt his own body react again. He wondered if he would come without even touching himself. Watching Willem would almost certainly be enough.

"In here." Willem took his hand again and led him into the bathroom. Closed the door, locked it, stood facing the sink, holding Richard back to front with an arm wrapped around his ribs. They gazed at each other in the mirror. "I understand there are things you think I won't like about you. I feel the same way about myself. There are things that are awful and I can't stand the thought that you might decide I'm not worth it. But Jesus help me, I can't not do this." His voice was shaking. He put both hands on Richard then, stroking down from his shoulders to his hands. Wrapping his fingers around Richard's wrists, dipping his head to press his mouth against Richard's neck. Absorbing the shudder that went through that wiry body.

Richard let his head rest against Willem's and raised his arms. Locked his hands behind Willem's neck and closed his eyes. Felt those hands on his chest, stroking down his sides to his hips. Felt the erection pressed against his ass and opened his legs a little. Willem made a sound and pulled them tight together. He slipped his thumbs under Richard's waistband, and then one hand was at his fly, opening his pants. "Oh God, Willem."

"I know." Both hands inside his pants, stroking down the front of his narrow hips, then one hand closing on Richard's cock. "Oh Jesus fuck." That hot silky length in his hand. He could feel Richard's heartbeat and it made his own heart race. His palm curved around the moist head, then stroked down, thumb hooked over the base as he cupped Richard's balls. "You're going to come for me."

Richard tried to remember to breathe. Must have been breathing, because he was saying things, but all he was really conscious of was Willem's hand on him, taking him to peak in a few confident strokes, then over the edge so fast, before he was ready, he didn't want this to end. He came hard, pulsing in Willem's hand. The sound Willem made was almost as loud as his own. He stood there, shaking, eyes still closed, and breathed deep.

"You are so beautiful." Willem's voice. "Now watch me."

Richard opened his eyes. He saw them both again in the mirror. Willem's other hand held the pink velvet shirt up, out of the danger zone. Richard hadn't even been aware of that hand. He reached for a paper towel and tidied up, then turned. "Will you let me?"

"Let you do what." Willem had his pants open now, hissing as he got himself free. "Jesus, I've never been so hard in my life. Fuck, no, I promise I'll let you someday, but God *damn*." Leaning over with one hand on the sink, the other working while Richard watched, standing close with his hand in Willem's hair. It was over in less than a minute. They both said "Oh God." Willem stood there, head down, panting.

After another minute Richard said, "Better?" Willem half-laughed, washed his hands, put himself together. Richard had himself in order too. "Let's say these horrible things." They went out and sat on the couch, close enough to touch.

"Can I say something that's not horrible first? I've been wanting to say this for weeks and I'm more scared of saying this than anything." Willem looked slightly pale now, as if he really were scared. Richard took his hand and nodded. "I love you."

Thank you Lord. "I love you too."

"Oh my *God* what a relief." They both leaned in, tipped their foreheads together for a moment, then leaned back. "Well. Maybe we'll survive this next part."

"I'll go first." Richard took a moment. "I've been hospitalized twice for anorexia and once for an overdose. I deal with anorexia every day, since I was thirteen. It took a long time for me to tell anyone aside from my shrink. I didn't even try to have a relationship for ten years. It's something I thought would kill me, something I'll always live with. Sometimes it's easy to manage, sometimes it's a roller coaster of anxiety and obsession and freakish behavior." He was shivering, as if he were cold.

But Willem was still holding his hand, and when Richard looked up there was nothing on that handsome face but concern and caring and love. "That's it?"

Richard's eyebrows went up. "Willem, it's kind of major."

An impatient shake of the head. "No, being a fugitive bank robber would be major. I knew you had some rituals but, you know, big deal. You seem healthy to me. You were hospitalized twice?" He would come back to the overdose some other time. He couldn't help thinking it was related to this other thing, which was obviously more important to Richard.

"The last time was more than ten years ago. I almost died. That's when my voice got broken. But after college I moved out here, and I found ballroom, and I have a good therapist. I still see him once a month. You really don't think this is a big thing?"

"Richard, you've seen how I eat most of the time. You've heard me bitch about what I can and cannot eat.

I always had to manage my calories down to the fucking decimal point because of how I have to look. I'm so obsessed with food I barely even noticed your thing. I'm not making light of it, I understand on your side it's a thing, but from my perspective it is not a problem. I don't know why anybody would think it's a problem, aside from wanting to be sure you're strong enough for me to fuck you." Richard almost laughed. "And the way you can dance, I honestly never thought that was going to be a problem. It wasn't a problem before, and you're stronger now. Wait." He was thinking. "Was it a problem? Did I hurt you? Or –"

Richard stopped him. "No, you didn't hurt me. You were perfect. I was a little messed up *about* you, but not *by* you."

Willem heard 'you were perfect' and told himself he'd cherish that later. "Did it start with that guy? The first guy." He was almost sure the answer would be yes. He was surprised to get a negative shake of the head. "What?"

"I was a child actor," Richard said, and saw instant comprehension. "We can talk about all that some more later. I'm so relieved. You're so normal. I didn't want to be the weak link."

Willem heard 'normal' and thought *oh shit*. "You won't be. I'm an alcoholic." Saying it felt easy now, or would have if the need for acceptance wasn't so strong.

"Yeah, I figured."

Willem blinked. "You what?" Richard leaned close again and kissed him lightly. Almost casually, as if he couldn't help himself but there was nothing else to be done. "You knew? I thought I was not so obvious."

"You're totally not obvious, but I grew up with an alcoholic. My mother is an alcoholic. I got addicted to not eating instead of to booze." Richard shrugged a little, almost apologetically.

"Well I'll be damned." Willem huffed out a laugh. "We're perfect for each other, aren't we." He performed a slow collapse onto the back cushion of the couch. Still holding Richard's hand.

Richard reclined too. They were turned toward each other, each with one knee up and one foot on the floor. He couldn't believe it was this easy. "So what happens now?"

"Do you want to keep going?"

"Yes, of course. Absolutely." He saw Willem relax, truly relax, and understood how very afraid he'd been. Even more than Richard, apparently. "We need to get to the bottom of your inferiority complex, Mr. van der Meer." Another breathy laugh from Willem. "But maybe not tonight."

"Back in the studio Wednesday? To finish 'Violet'? I love what we're doing."

"I love it too." They both seemed to accept that the last two statements encompassed much more than dancing. "Let's put this couch back where it belongs." They waited until they were back out on the club floor before indulging in a proper kiss. They both thought it was funny. "That was something we needed," Richard said after they separated. "All of that. You still want to wait?" He meant 'for more.'

"I kind of do." Willem couldn't have said why, except that for most of two months they'd been concentrating on each other as people, not simply as lovers, and they'd gotten to a place he'd never been before. "It'll be easier now, won't it?"

"Now that we can kiss good night and say I love you? I think so." Richard leaned in to kiss him again.

"I won't promise not to make a pass at you. Or to tell you things I wish we were doing."

"I've got a really long list of those." They grinned at each other. "Let's get out of here, it's a work night."

Chapter 15

The next rehearsal was all 'Violet.' They'd been working on it here and there since the beginning of January, they'd just put it on video for submission, and there was only one problem. Richard looked up at Willem from his position on the floor and said, "I'm having a little trouble with impostor syndrome."

Willem flopped down beside him and mirrored his stretch. "Me too. I've never made my own choreography before, not something like this. December was the closest."

"And until December I've never done it at all, outside of stringing a phrase together for a class I'm teaching. When I did that thing with Mateo it was him and Dmitri and Julia." They gazed at each other thoughtfully. Richard wasn't sure this was a great idea, but it wouldn't go away. "What would you think of taking it to the jazz crew?"

"Do you think they would mind?" Willem hadn't tried to insert himself into that activity. He knew how much Richard cherished it, and he still worried about overdoing things.

Richard shook his head. "I think they'd be glad to comment on it. They all know you, it's not like I'd be dragging some stranger in there." He tried to gauge Willem's feelings. "I'd love for you to join us anytime. I'm sure they'd be happy to have you there. Only if you want to, though." Willem was bent over a leg. He turned his head to look at Richard, who couldn't read his expression. "I really want them to see us do this. I never thought I could do something like this." Trying to make it about him, except he couldn't, it wouldn't be true. "I never would have tried if it weren't for you."

Willem sat up. "Oh, sure you would. Mateo would have talked you into something sometime." He saw Richard's reflexive movement, a subtle rejection, and suddenly thought *Or no, because something awful might have happened.* It was so easy to forget Richard had this thing he struggled with. It was so much tougher than Willem's thing, because it was something he had to do rather than something he had to avoid. "I'd love for them to see it," he confessed. "I kind of forgot I've danced with all of them, except Rory, and she's the coolest."

"She is." Richard scooted closer and did the thing they did now when they were alone. A moment of contact, cheek to cheek. Not a kiss but with the same intention. Not otherwise touching, because the desire was always there, always smoldering, all too readily fanned into open flame. He stayed close for a breath, then moved away to find his phone. Sent a text, stretched for a few more minutes, then got to his feet. He thought he had enough fuel left to go one more time, but it would be wiser to stop before he was completely wrung out. "I'll let you know what she says. It'll be next Wednesday if it's a go."

"I'll be available." Willem stood up. "Could you do me a favor? I want to get something at the Italian joint before they close, could you make sure I don't order tiramisu?"

You don't fool me, Richard thought, and said, "Of course." It wasn't at all surprising that he ended up eating most of the caprese they allegedly got to share, and it also wasn't surprising that before they left the restaurant Rory texted back to say *BRING IT.*

With a potentially exhausting evening ahead of him, Richard did something he generally tried not to do, and took a dose of an anti-anxiety medication Dr. Simon prescribed. It was known to be habit-forming, so they both considered it a preventive measure for unusually challenging situations, if not a last resort. With that in his system, it was easier to mute the disorder. Which made it possible to eat half of a giant, protein-packed Cobb salad for lunch and the other half before going home to change for the jazz class. Rory had already told him she would bring snacks – as she often did – and he knew everyone there would be wolfing down whatever it was. He'd be able to eat something more then. It was infuriating that this was still a thing, that his intellectual grasp of the disorder was so inadequate to mastering it. *Logic does not win against emotion*, he told himself for the millionth time.

And when he saw Willem that night he was glad it didn't. If he went with logic he might still be alone instead of about to step into a rehearsal room with this beautiful man and seven other friends. They took a minute or five to hug and kiss before going in. It was actually eight more friends, Richard saw when the door opened; Vicky was there too. "I heard another of our Great Wavers would be here tonight and Sharon needed some quiet time, so hi," she said. Willem shook her hand and said he was glad to see her. Everyone else exchanged greetings, and there was some chatter about what was happening for the next show. The only person there who didn't have a routine going in was Vicky, who bitched about it for a minute before heaving a sigh. "It's my own fault," she said. "I could have gotten Hiro if I'd said something at the right moment."

"You can tell us all what we're fucking up," Mateo said. "Crack the whip, Glamazon."

It turned into a proper rehearsal. Everybody worked hard, but with so many routines to review

Richard didn't get worn out. Ann and Bonnie shut it down five minutes before the hour was up. "So guys, was there something you wanted input for? Because frankly I think you're ready to go." Ann was speaking to Richard and Willem, but she looked around at everyone else, soliciting disagreement that didn't come.

"Righteous work," Bonnie said. "Glad we got to see it in advance. That song gives me chills."

"For real." Paula was on the floor stretching. "That was one of my standbys when I was at peak rage." All the women laughed; they knew about Paula's rage. Then everyone looked at Willem and Richard, as if wondering about theirs.

"We have some issues," Richard said after a moment. "Both of us. And we haven't done work like this before, so we wanted some objective opinions. It occurs to me that this might not be the right place to get those."

Rory said, "Oh, we would tell you if it sucked. It does not suck. Don't change anything. Let's go out in the waiting room and I'll open the feed bag."

An hour later, Richard was parked behind Willem on a side street a few blocks from the dance studio. "Thanks for giving me a lift," Willem said.

"Anything for a few more minutes with you. Did you think they'd all say, well okay but, and then have a bunch of suggestions?"

Willem laughed under his breath. "I kind of did. When we ran it on video last week it still looked so raw. Maybe that's what it needs, though."

"It feels so … transgressive. Doesn't it? Like, you're not supposed to say these things."

Willem took his hand, stroking a thumb lightly over the back. "Did you ever scream at your mother?"

"No, I never did. Maybe that's what this is. Screaming at her, and at that guy, and at anorexia." He didn't always name it. Maybe he should. "Who didn't you scream at?"

"Oh … everybody. I'm pretty sure I need therapy." Willem tried to make that sound like a joke.

"You never had any?" Richard couldn't believe it. He didn't know anyone who'd stayed sober without therapy. "You know you can tell me anything. Everything."

Not everything. "You don't need to carry my baggage."

Richard leaned close to press his cheek to Willem's. "That's not how it works. You talk about it to unpack it. It really works, you know. Sometimes it takes a while. But baggage only gets heavier if you don't talk. Trust me." He sat back a little. "Are you all right?"

"I'm fine. I will be fine," Willem clarified. "This number does stir up some shit. Anyway. You are great, and I love you, and I'd better get out of this car."

"I love you too. Text me when you get home." Willem let go of his hand and opened the door. Swung one leg out and then lunged back across for a fast, hard kiss before exiting the vehicle. Richard was laughing. "Cheater."

"Quit being so perfect and I'll resist you better. Drive safe." Willem closed the door and stood on the sidewalk for a few seconds, as if to make sure he had his shoe bag and whatever, before turning toward his car. Richard waited till he was inside before starting his engine and pulling away from the curb. Wishing, as he did more intensely by the week, that they were going home together.

Willem was dividing his time between the ballet studio (a group class six days a week), a private training gym (an average of three sessions a day), and a yoga studio that was not Tidal Flow (two more group classes). The three locations were within a few minutes' drive of each other, which made his days relatively low-stress. And now every day ended with some kind of contact with Richard, a text or call, always including an 'I love you.' It was intoxicating and a little frightening.

They met at least once a week to work on their dances for the Cabaret, and met for dinner at least twice a week. The only reason he didn't suggest spending Sunday afternoons together was a lingering fear of relying too much on one person, especially on this person. It wasn't that he thought Richard would turn on him, or turn away. It was this feeling that once the novelty wore off, Richard would see that there wasn't much to him. Willem wanted to delay that day as long as possible.

He was still in touch with Karen; they met up for class as usual once a week. He told her all about what was happening with Richard. She said she was happy for him. Then midway through February, when he was a little distracted by the need to polish up their Cabaret routine, she said, "We need to talk."

That tone was unmistakable. If they'd been dating he would instantly have thought *oh shit*. Since they weren't, he said, "What's wrong?"

"Rhonda asked me to develop a group class called yoga for dancers."

It was so crass, he almost laughed. "Somehow I'm not surprised. What did you tell her? I don't own the concept."

"I told her I'd pitch her something in a week or so. I wanted to tell you, and I wanted to come to your class because I don't want to do the same class. I almost told her no. I almost said, you had that guy right here." She looked annoyed. "She doesn't know we're friends. Can you believe that? If Kevin and I didn't spend so much time together, she probably wouldn't have caught on to that. Way back when he and I were getting acquainted we both said, the thing we dislike about this place is lousy team-building. It's because that ridiculous woman doesn't pay attention."

"No, she doesn't. But that's enough about her." Willem dismissed it. It was a non-problem. "Of course you can come to my class and of course I wouldn't care if you stole the whole thing. Everybody's got a different way. Some people who struggle in my class will probably do great with you, and I will send them to you."

"You are a righteous dude, Willem, and don't let anybody tell you different. I hope you know the exact same thing applies on my side." She looked away for a minute, then back at him, and sighed. "Rhonda also offered me a full-time position there. With benefits."

"Oh, okay, she's a bitch." He leaned against the wall, laughing.

Karen cracked up too. "Oh my God I *know*. I didn't know what to say." She edged closer to bump her shoulder against Willem. "I'll probably say no. It would be nice to have someone help me pay for health insurance, but I kind of don't want to be tied to her."

He put his arm around her shoulders and kissed her forehead. "I said something mean about you last fall.

When I asked her about going full time. I said I don't have a trust fund. It wasn't fair."

She slid her arm around his waist and leaned against him. "It's okay. It's a valid point. I know you know I'd rather have my family back." Karen's 'trust fund' was the result of a highway accident that cost her both parents and her brother. "And I know they'd rather I didn't get stuck in some crappy job because I was afraid of losing a few bucks." She tipped her head up to make eye contact. "Are you and Richard going to get married? He's got a fat office job, right? Probably has great bennies."

It made him laugh all over again. "He probably does, he does, and I don't know. We are not there yet. I haven't told a guy I loved him since I was seventeen. I am freaked way the hell out."

"Oh God, I can imagine, I haven't told a guy that for that long either. Wow, we are a pair of winners, aren't we?" She patted his back. "But he loves you. I can't wait to see the next dance. Which of you chose that track?"

"I did, after he told me some stuff. Karen, I don't know what I'm going to do if this goes wrong." He didn't know where that came from. All of a sudden his breath was short and his eyes were wet. She didn't say anything, simply turned toward him and hugged him. He wrapped his arms around her and rested his cheek on her hair.

After what seemed like forever, when he wasn't struggling to breathe anymore, she said, "Did you change your life for him, or for you?"

Willem thought about it for half a minute. "For me. I think I always hoped he would be there somewhere, but it was for me."

"Then you're going to be okay, no matter what. Hey." She made him look at her. "You are a good person. A smart, talented, special person. You are going to be okay."

He kissed her lightly on the mouth. "Thank you. Back at ya. We are so late for class."

"Yes we are. Come on."

The reaction to their audition video for 'Violet' might have been different if the Underground Cabaret principals didn't all know Richard and Willem by now. Because they did, everyone but Rory wanted to know 'WTF where did this come from.' They didn't know if they should try to answer that, or if it was one of those things that looked like a question but didn't require a response. In the end, they went with the second interpretation. Consequently, they spent a good bit of time after the dress rehearsal giving variations on Richard's comment to the jazz crew: we both have some issues. They dodged the few follow-up questions and steered people into discussions of their own routines.

"This fucking show is like a group therapy session," Rory said after a while. The traditional post-dress pizzas had been demolished, a number of the performers had already left, and the rest of them were sitting around the downstairs lounge at Chrome, variously tired or rattled or sore. "Who chose this bananapants theme, anyway?"

"Uh," said Mateo, "I think that was you."

Richard nodded sadly. "I'm sorry, Rory. It was you. I distinctly remember you saying, these February shows are supposed to hook into Valentine's Day, last year we got our heads twisted off, let's do something that'll rock this joint and really make people buy drinks. Heart Shaped Box, you said. It'll be fun, you said. It was you."

Rory elbowed Dana, who was cracking up. "You would think by now I wouldn't be surprised by the sick shit you people come up with."

"Look who's talking," Anya said. "Who does a mostly-naked jazz routine to 'Loser' except you?"

"Best stripper in L.A. two years running," Rory reminded her, and took a drink.

"Anyway, it's a good show." Dana stood up and stretched. "Really great stuff from everybody. And drinks will be sold. Richard, Terry came up with a new cocktail based on your number."

"Jesus, no," Willem said. "What's in it? Squid ink and razor blades?"

"Crème de Cassis and lavender gin, with one of those ice things that has a hole through the middle," Anya said. "Garnished with a candied violet that's been hit with a torch."

"Good Lord," Richard said. "I may have to try that. Is it time to go, honey?"

Willem glanced at his phone and sighed. "Yeah. I need to get over to the gym. Drop me back at Mandy's?" They collected their gear, said their goodbyes, and made their way upstairs. "Still feeling good about it?"

"I think I'm more worn out from talking than from the number," Richard said as they got into his car.

"You felt really solid today. Resilient. Is it my imagination or have you gotten stronger?"

"I might have." Richard glanced over. "I've put on a little weight."

"I thought so! Didn't want to say anything. That's good, right? It has to be all muscle." Willem was thrilled.

"I'm going in for a physical next week." Richard was smiling. That happy note in Willem's voice was the best. "It'll be interesting to see what the cardiac assessment says. You know I was doing all that low-intensity stuff for a long time."

"This shit is not low-intensity." Richard snorted. Willem grinned over at him. "I was knocked out, frankly. I knew you were tough but you've got more power than I expected."

"You think I'm tough?"

"Duh, yeah. You're a survivor. I'll tell you what I really love about this one." Richard waited, then made an inquiring sound. Willem was putting his thoughts in order. After a minute he said, "It's that the things we do in the solos are very individual, but on the synched phrases we get such unison. Obviously everything's not the same size, because I'm taller. But your timing and your speed, your rotation and axis and extension, are just really fucking good and we look *together*. We are together. We look like we're saying the same thing."

Richard swallowed and took a breath. "I never would have thought I could even keep up with you. This is all so … beyond."

"Yeah. I know." They were both talking about more than the dancing. "I like what we're doing with the next one, too. That West Coast swing stuff."

"It works great with Broadway-style jazz, doesn't it?" Richard was pleased with the way their routine for 'Speakeasy' was coming along. He'd chosen the music again, 'Mood Indigo' from the soundtrack of 'The Cotton Club.' It was completely different from the other two routines. Without the rage-driven energy of 'Violet,' slinky and sexy in a way 'Trail of Broken Hearts' hadn't been. Their three dances seemed to be reflecting the progress of their relationship. He wasn't sure they even needed to talk again after the March show. He was hoping all they needed to do was kiss. In private.

They did some very good kissing in Mandy's parking lot. So good that neither of them wanted to call it a day. At least three drivers honked as they went past. "God, this is torture," Willem said. He was leaning against his car with Richard in his arms. "Whose idea was this anyway?"

"Yours." Richard's tone left no doubt that his agreement to the deal was revocable. Willem laughed into his hair. Richard spoke against Willem's throat. "If you're planning to meet your client at the gym, you'd better let go of me." He made no effort to move away.

Fuck that client, Willem thought, but reluctantly opened his arms. "I would rather stand here with you till sunset," he said, "but you have a date with Sam and Mateo. Don't do anything I wouldn't do. Oh wait." Richard laughed. Willem kissed him again. "Tell them I love their number." Another kiss. "I love you."

"I love you too." One more kiss, and Richard stepped away.

Chapter 16

Finishing that dance should have been an unqualified good. They were in the homestretch now, and Willem didn't think it was possible to be more in love than he was. He believed that Richard loved him too. It wasn't only that they said it to each other, it was the way they moved and touched and kissed. The way even disagreement (always over something trivial, like what to do in the next sixteen bars of music or whether they'd been to the Italian place too often recently) wasn't stressful. So it was ridiculous not to be completely happy. The fact that he hadn't been completely happy for nearly thirty years should have been irrelevant.

It was Mandy and Karen who brought up the subject of anxiety, and they did it close enough together that Willem couldn't help thinking of it as a single conversation. On the same day, in fact, which meant his cover was slipping. He looked at Karen over his coffee cup and set it down again without taking a sip. "Why do you think I'm not happy?"

"I don't think you're not happy," she said carefully. "But I think there's something bothering you. If I hadn't known you for a year I wouldn't notice. If we weren't friends. But I have, and we are, and what's up."

He did not, not, not want to have this conversation. He felt that mental gate clang shut, even though he knew she wasn't attacking. Karen was not the person who would say 'what's bothering you' meaning 'what's wrong with you.' But he'd heard that a lot. He never stopped hearing it. Even now, when he was the one in charge and hardly anybody questioned him. He couldn't help waiting for the other shoe to drop. For everyone to suddenly recognize that he didn't know what he was doing, he wasn't any good, this was all some kind of accident. A cosmic joke. He thought he'd said something, so he was surprised when Karen put her hand on his arm and said, "Willem?"

Her tone was sufficiently concerned that he blinked, and sucked in a breath that was slightly overdue. A few slower, deeper, calmer breaths later he said, "I'm okay. There have been a lot of changes this year. All good, but I'm still adjusting. That's all."

She looked unconvinced. Took a sip of her tea and sat there studying him. "Have you done a restorative practice lately?"

"Eh … not for a while. Not one I wasn't leading," he admitted.

"Are you seeing Richard tonight?" He shook his head. Karen said, "Then send him a text and let's hang out here. Mandy doesn't have anyone in the private room for the next half hour. Let's see if I can chill you out."

He didn't argue. He was too grateful. "Okay." He sent a text, as directed: *Hanging out with the gal pal for a while. Wanted to kiss you goodnight before it gets too late. I love you XOX*

A reply came in quickly: *I love you too. Say hi to Karen for me. See you tomorrow sweetheart XOX.* Willem read it three times, wishing it were already tomorrow. "Richard says hi."

"You know you can tell me anything."

He really couldn't. What she could hear and what he could say were, he suspected, very different things. "I love you too. Let's go chill out." He could tell she wasn't a hundred percent satisfied with that, but she only made a growly sound and headed down the hall.

When he got home, Willem updated his calendar, dealt with his email, and took care of other bits of accumulated business while he ate his take-out dinner. At least in L.A. you could get healthy take-out at pretty much any hour. After tidying up his room he sat for a while staring at it. He was close to escape velocity, close to feeling financially ready to make a move. He needed to talk to Richard about it. Maybe that was why he was giving off a whiff of anxiety.

Now that he thought about it, neither Mandy nor Karen had used that word. They'd asked, is everything all right, are you happy with the way things are going. It was his mind that supplied the A word. He knew perfectly well why. This had happened before, and he'd let it spill over into his then-relationship, with predictable results. He needed to box it up. His issues were not Richard's problem. His lover (soon to be, please God) had his own issues to cope with, and he was coping magnificently. If Willem ever let this shit out, it might knock Richard out of equilibrium. And he knew he was going to hear 'you need therapy.' Maybe it would help, but maybe it wouldn't, and then he'd have gone through that for nothing. He might re-live all the things he could mostly manage not to think about, bring them out into the light, and then maybe find he couldn't get them back in the box. Then what would happen to Richard? To *them*?

He wanted to be in love. That was all he wanted. It didn't seem like so much to ask. And now that he had it, he didn't want to screw it up. *That isn't all you want*, some small dark voice whispered. He wanted to live with Richard. Wanted to marry Richard. Could he possibly deserve that, could he even ask for it, when

Richard didn't know everything? "Stop it," he said out loud. His body was so tense, that half-hour with Karen might never have happened.

Two weeks after 'Heart Shaped Box' Richard was over at Rory and Dana's again, going through the submissions for 'Speakeasy.' The show was almost full now that they had the thing Rory was doing with her new discovery. That routine wasn't fully polished, but everyone who saw it said 'hey now' and the vote was unanimous. "How did you find this Zach guy?"

"He found me. He was at the last show and pinned me down at the bar and propositioned me." Rory elbowed Dana, who was laughing. "Told me who he was and where he teaches, what styles he does, and then proposed that track and I was like, you got me. He is a beast. I wanted to ask if you had any fallout from your number."

Richard knew what she meant. "A little. My whole thing is about control, so doing something where I let myself lose it was very scary. Plus it's the most physically demanding thing I've done in roughly two decades. Willem was checking in with me constantly. He's like you. He can do it so all that comes across is concern, not criticism. It's probably one reason he got so successful so fast as an instructor."

Dana swirled the wine around in her glass, looking thoughtful. "Does he realize what a success he is? I get the feeling maybe he doesn't, but maybe I'm missing something."

"No, I think you're right." Richard leaned back. Immediately the cat was on his lap. "Hi Spike. Yes I know, I'm sorry my lap isn't wider. Settle down." He waited patiently for the cat to accept the limitations of this lap, then sank his hand into all that fur. "There was a moment last week when I had that thought. We were over at Sam and Mateo's and got talking about our day jobs for a change. Both of those guys, you wouldn't think they do what they do. An ex-fighter who's a fashion guru? And Mateo being a draftsman, well, I guess as creative as he is that does make sense. I just can't imagine him sitting still at a computer for very long." Rory snorted. "Me on the other hand, with my control issues, I fell into the perfect job. Keeping files organized, yep, I'm your man."

"And then there's Willem, who is kind of a mystery. He doesn't talk about himself much. When did he start in showbiz?" The question sounded idle, but Dana had an idea and wanted to see if she was on track.

"He was getting cast in local things when he was a kid. Some of the same things I did. 'Oliver,' 'Annie,' 'Sound of Music.' He did 'Nutcracker' too, a bunch of times. His parents let him take jobs in Chicago as soon as he could drive. He played Lun Tha in 'The King and I' when he was eighteen. I wish I could have seen that." Richard heard the wistful note in his voice and got back on track. "He was working all through college, which he says was because he wanted a safety net. Getting the degree would look good when he had to stop dancing. Then three years in New York, fully employed, before coming out here with a boyfriend. He says they broke up within a year and the other guy went back East. He met Robbie Campbell somehow and stayed because of that benefit, and after that he was getting cast pretty regularly in things so he kept not leaving. That's how he put it." He took a sip of wine, thinking about how Willem seemed to believe his twenty-plus years on stage didn't amount to anything.

Rory was staring at him. "He's a little conflicted, isn't he? All that time he was piling up all those credits, and he got the yoga certification."

"And a personal trainer certification. I think someone sometime must have convinced him that what he was doing wasn't a real job. Didn't have value. I hope it wasn't his parents, but his brother is a lawyer and his sister is a nurse. They're both younger. I have this awful suspicion that there might have been one of those 'thank God these two are normal' things."

Dana said, "You never got that."

"No, because my brother is even more messed up than I am. By the time I started having trouble he was already in rehab." Richard drank a little more wine, set down the glass, and buried both hands in Spike's fur. "I'm not the right person to tell Willem he didn't waste those years. I'm younger, and I quit before I was even an adult. What we have is so good, and it's getting better, but I'm afraid he'll never be happy because he feels like he failed." He was afraid there was more to it, actually, but this was all he could bring himself to say.

"For fuck's sake," said Rory. "If that's what failure looks like I should take a long walk off a short pier immediately. Dana, do you think maybe Andy?"

It sounded like an incomplete question, but Dana seemed to know exactly what Rory meant. "I'll ask him."

Richard wasn't sure where Rory and Dana were going with the 'maybe Andy' thing, and he didn't want to wait for that to play out. He and Willem were so good together, and the other man's business was going so well, but it seemed as though his anxiety was getting worse. He was putting all his energy into other people, instead of himself. Deflecting even the most non-specific expressions of concern. Richard couldn't help fearing it would get to be too much.

He was sufficiently worried that he brought it up in his next therapy session. "We've been using these dances to work through our issues. It wasn't really intentional, but I guess sometimes the work takes you where you need to go. On my side, it's been nothing but positive. But I'm afraid it's hurting Willem."

Dr. Simon asked a few questions, made a few notes, then stared into space for a few minutes. Tapping his notepad with his pen. Richard waited. Eventually the psychiatrist made a suggestion. "This is, arguably, outside the lines. If the two of you hadn't made certain representations of the long-term-commitment variety, I wouldn't suggest it. And of course just because I suggest it doesn't mean you should do it."

Richard waited for the rest. "Well, what is it?"

The counselor answered indirectly. "Have you spoken to anyone in his family?"

"Only on Facebook. His brother and sister comment on our stuff. We've all done the friends thing."

"Then they know who you are. Do you get the sense that Willem talks openly with them?"

"I think he absolutely doesn't. I think he's been protecting them all their lives." And he had no idea why.

"Would they help if they thought he needed it?"

"I'm pretty sure they would. You think I should get them out here, don't you." Dr. Simon made a 'maybe?' face. Richard considered it. Organizing what amounted to an intervention was fraught with potential for disaster. It could completely torpedo their relationship. On the other hand, it was increasingly clear that love was not enough. Everything that was going right was tied somehow, in Willem's mind, to something very wrong, and Richard didn't know what it was. Willem consistently deflected, avoided, distracted. He realized he'd been silent for quite some time. "He's an alcoholic." He hadn't told Dr. Simon this before. "He's been sober for nine years. I don't know anything about how long he had a problem, or how it started, or why."

"He doesn't talk to you."

"Not about that."

Dr. Simon nodded, with a small sigh. "The question, of course, is are you prepared to accept the consequences."

Richard didn't have to think about that for long. "If I have to lose him, I would rather it was because I tried to help than because I didn't."

"You think it's that serious?"

"I don't *know*. All I know is he's so smart, and so strong, but something is broken."

Dr. Simon sat back, re-crossed his legs, tapped his notepad with his pen. "I wish you were married so I could get you both in here. Well, I trust you to do what you think is right. Now. How are you?"

"I'm better. Not cured, but better. Ironic, isn't it? Maybe all I needed was to get out of my own head."

"Say that when you're cured," was the therapist's advice.

At home that night, Richard debated for nearly an hour before sending a PM to Willem's brother: *Hi Laurence I need your advice about something I don't want going through FB. Would you mind if I send you an email?*

A reply came fast: *Not at all here's my address*

Armed with that, Richard composed a fairly lengthy letter. He didn't want to overstate the problem, and admitted he wasn't sure of his footing. It was this increasingly strong sense of something amiss, and fear that he wasn't equipped to give Willem the help he might need. He edited as little as possible because he wanted to get the thing out the door before he lost his nerve. After it was sent he felt shaky, and realized he hadn't eaten. *Fucking food*, he thought with such uncharacteristic irritation that he almost laughed. He employed some more uncharacteristic profanity while he assembled dinner. It took him a while to eat all of it, but he did. Then he sent a text to Willem: *Hi sweetheart. Doc Simon was good today. Did you go to class with Karen? Just finished dinner and wanted to kiss you goodnight. I love you XOX*

Willem's reply pinged in while Richard was brushing his teeth: *Hi gorgeous, I love you too. Yes we did class and she told me about some more stupid shit Rhonda is doing. When do I see you again? XOX*

Sunday morning seems too far away

Very true. Do we need to practice?

I always need to practice

LOL no you don't but let me ping Mandy and see if her private room is available anytime Saturday. Uh does any time work for you?

Yes it does. Get some sleep honey I know you have a heavy day tomorrow

Ugh Fridays okay. Love you

Love you too. Richard half-hoped there would be another message. Wished they were together. Missed Willem so much he ached with it. If they made it to the end of 'Speakeasy' – made it in every sense – he hoped they would never have to miss each other again.

He had a reply from Laurence in the morning.

> Richard – thanks for your letter. I talked to Steph and she says she hasn't heard much from our brother lately. We appreciate you reaching out. He is not good at showing weakness. If he is letting some cracks show with you he must really trust you, which makes us think you must a) know him very well and b) care about him a lot. We know you have a show coming up. We know he has never missed a show except when he had an actual broken bone, so we're going to be in LA the weekend after and we'll get to the bottom of this. A hotel room might be a good neutral setting. If you have some friends to help out that would be great. We haven't tried to pin him down for a long time and he's a slippery son of a gun. Will be in touch with ETA etc. Thanks again – Laurence

Chapter 17

Willem was fully astonished to get a PM from his brother saying both his siblings were coming out to Los Angeles the weekend after 'Speakeasy.' They'd never visited before; he'd only seen them when he went home. Not that Urbana was really home. When he asked what the occasion was, Laurence replied *haven't seen you in approximately forever and want to meet Richard. If you didn't want us to be burning up with curiosity you shouldn't have been posting all that shit.* It made Willem laugh. And knowing he would see them – here, on his own turf, where none of the bad memories lived – made him happy. "The only thing wrong with this plan," he told Richard on the phone, "is I was planning to spend that whole weekend in bed with you." The very thought of it turned him on.

"We could both take the day off after 'Speakeasy,'" Richard suggested. "Would that help?"

"Jesus, yes. I still think it was good to wait but I still hate myself every day. Every night, especially." Richard laughed. Willem wished they were in the same room so he could see that. "One or the other of us is going to be late for work a lot for a while."

Richard was still smiling when he answered. "You should move in with me. It would solve so many problems."

Willem couldn't speak for a moment. That was in the category of wonderful things he wished would happen that he was not sure he would ever have had the nerve to ask for. "Are you serious?"

"Of course I'm serious. I love you. We only slept together that one time, but it's all I think about."

Richard listened to the silence at the other end, hoping it was for a good reason. "Willem?"

"I love you too. Let's talk about this again soon. Right now I'm stuck on how we slept together that one time." It was true, if not the whole truth. "And how we made love those other two times." Still not the whole truth. "And how I'm dying to make love with you again now that you know I love you."

"God, Willem, I wish you were here right now."

"Are you going to get yourself off tonight?"

"I'm halfway there already."

"Me too. See you for practice."

"I love you. Good night."

"Good night, gorgeous. I love you." He had to say it again. Then he disconnected before he could actually lose his shit and either start crying or say 'the hell with it, this can't possibly go wrong, I'm on my way over.' Because of course it could still go wrong. But for now he was going to put that out of his mind and put a picture of Richard there instead.

The March edition of Mating Dance was, Richard thought, the best yet, and not only because he and Willem were dancing again. 'Speakeasy' opened with Rory and Zach's unbelievable cabaret jazz quickstep Charleston mash-up and closed with the first legit ballet pas de deux in Underground Cabaret history. That was courtesy of Mike and Paula Borodin, doing a piece adapted from 'The Golden Age.' If he and Willem hadn't both been slightly impatient to get out of there, they would have been happy to hang around the after-party to talk about the ballet piece, and to interrogate Willem's friend Karen about Zach. The two of them were at a table and it seemed they had an awful lot to say to each other. “He’s the guy she chucked out of her yoga class three years ago,” Willem told Richard on their way out. “And now they’re working up something for the May showcase. She won’t tell me what it is.”

“All you dance people.” Richard couldn’t keep the amusement out of his tone. “Can’t stay away from it.”

“What do you mean, all *you* dance people.” He held the door, they left the building, they headed toward Willem’s car. He was more nervous now than he had been before they went onstage. Their jazzy swing was so well-rehearsed (and, he acknowledged, so well-constructed) it felt more like lead-and-follow than choreography. Now they were all out of choreography, and heading into something he had no idea how to lead. “Did you hear what the pro-show director said to me?”

Richard glanced over at Willem as they got into the car. “I saw her, but when she was talking to Dmitri. I didn’t want to interrupt. What did she say?”

“She said, you two are really showing up in these routines, I’d love to see something from you for this year’s concert.” Willem didn’t start the car yet; he wanted to see Richard’s reaction to this, which was wide-eyed surprise. It made him smile. “She hasn’t posted about it yet. Nobody seems to know what she’s doing.”

Richard finally found speech again. “No. A lot of her regulars aren’t going to be available this summer. A whole mob is going to Paris for the Gay Games.” He buckled in. Willem started the car. They were well out of Hollywood before he said, “Would you want to try out for it?”

“Sure. I would have loved to do any and all of those pro shows. The one I was in was a great experience. Doing these numbers with you, well. It kind of lit me up again for dancing. It's not like doing a Broadway show, but that's not necessarily a bad thing." Richard snorted, a half-laugh of agreement. "I mean, not every song is 'We Kiss in a Shadow.' Oh my God I'd love to dance that with you." Willem glanced over, smiling. "I keep thinking of things I want to do with you."

"So do I." They were only a few minutes from his place now, and the things Richard was thinking of had nothing to do with being onstage. They hadn't even kissed at Chrome because tonight they were finally going to kiss in private again. Kissing in public seemed not precisely a waste of time, but surplus to requirements. "The first thing I want to do is take your clothes off." Willem exhaled audibly. "I want to see you naked in candlelight."

Mild, anticipatory excitement to full arousal in two seconds. Willem felt lightheaded. "Jesus, Richard, I'm trying to drive here."

"I want to touch you all over. I want to kiss you all over." He didn't know why he was doing this, but he kept going, itemizing all the places he wanted to kiss, and for how long, and whether he was going to lick or bite or suck while he was at it. Willem was breathing through his mouth and Richard had to adjust himself, shifting in his seat, because he was so turned on. "I want you in my mouth. God, I can almost taste you. I want you in me."

"*Richard.*" Willem was trying to find a parking place where he could leave the car all night, trying not to listen, trying not to actually crash. Trying not to notice Richard's head tipped back, eyes closed, hands gripping the tops of his thighs with his thumbs digging in. He found a parking spot, barely big enough for the

CRV. Took his time parking because the last thing he needed was to ding the car in front or behind.

As soon as the engine was off he was out of the car, thanking whatever gods might be listening that he'd planned ahead. Packed an overnight bag and sent it home with Richard after dress rehearsal, because he suspected one or both of them might not be in their right minds tonight. Richard was out of the car too. Willem closed the passenger door, clicked the remote to lock it, and wrapped an arm around Richard. They were two blocks from his apartment. If Willem kissed him anywhere along the way they were not going to make it. Richard's arm was around him, too, thumb stroking the bottom of his ribcage. They were both walking fast.

Finally they were at the building. Richard coded them in. They bypassed the elevator and went up the stairs to the third floor, then down the hall. Richard's hand was shaking as he put the key in the lock. Then they were inside, the door was closed, and his back was against the wall. Willem's tongue was in his mouth and their hands were everywhere, getting the bare minimum of necessary access to skin. It was not calm, not organized, not pretty. And it was Richard in Willem's mouth first, Willem on his knees with Richard's hands in his hair.

The night before, Willem had fantasized about taking his time with this, savoring every centimeter of skin, teasing and petting. He'd take his time later. At this moment there was nothing to be done but use his hand and his mouth to bring the climax as fast as possible. He needed to taste it, needed to see it happen. Needed to hear Richard, who hardly ever cursed, saying the loudest, filthiest things as he thrust forward, coming deep in Willem's throat with "Oh fucking *Christ*."

A moment of stillness, then Willem swallowed. Richard's body jerked again. He was leaning on the wall, panting, eyes closed. Willem stood up and kissed him, pushing into him. It was as if Richard's orgasm calmed his own storm. He was still aroused to the point of pain, but now he could control it. He dipped his head and spoke against Richard's throat. "I love you."

"I love you too." The hoarse voice was faint. Richard knew Willem would hear his smile. "Please tell me you're not done."

"I haven't even started." He moved against Richard again. "How do you want me."

"In the bedroom. On my bed. In me." He liked to take it from behind, or at least that was how he'd liked it with Willem before. The scene was already set; he'd seen to that earlier in the day. As soon as they were in there, clothes were coming off. Richard lit a candle with a hand that was barely trembling anymore. Then he ran his hands over Willem's glorious body, kissed him, tasted him, taking his time. They were here at last, together at last, with nothing but time. And thanks to that round of tests, they'd be skin to skin all the way through.

He listened to Willem's breath as he moved with Richard's touch. On his front, on his back, kneeling for a kiss. On hands and knees over Richard, eyes closed, lips parted, breath coming short. Richard used his hands and mouth to urge Willem past that point of calm, and back into the storm. Used his own body weight to push his lover up and away, because he couldn't wait any more.

Richard stood up, lifted the lube from the nightstand and put it in Willem's hand. "Now." He turned his back and braced one knee on the bed. Willem was on his feet. Richard felt a hand between his legs a second later, a caress, then pressure with the lube. Widened his stance and put his hands down. Willem's other hand sweeping down his back, around his ribs, over his chest. Playing with his nipple as a finger went in. "God almighty, Willem, fuck me *now*."

Willem held him steady. Slicked himself, pressed, pushed. "Oh my God, Richard. Holy fucking hell, Jesus, yes." He wanted to close his eyes so he could concentrate on the sensation, but he couldn't stand not to watch himself enter. Watching the muscles of Richard's back engage as he gave resistance. Watching his neck arch, then turn slightly, his eyes closing, lips parting. "You're so fucking beautiful."

"More. Oh *Christ* yes. Willem." Bracing himself, head dropping now, back flexing with Willem's thrusts.

"Are you hard again?" Willem reached around. "Jesus *fuck* I love you. Again. Again." He was going, going, he wanted everything, all of it, "Now, Richard, God!" Richard bucked under him with another curse, spilling in his hand, and Willem went with him.

A few minutes later, lying close together, Willem stirred. "Can you eat in bed?" There wasn't a verbal response, only a slight movement. "No, too chaotic. Okay. Quick shower, then sushi at the table like civilized people." He pushed himself up, got his feet on the floor, and gave Richard a hand. They both needed a moment to get their balance. "My God. Everything I imagined didn't quite add up to that."

Richard laughed under his breath as they moved toward the bathroom. "I don't know when I got such a filthy mouth. Maybe hanging around with Mateo." Willem snorted. "You liked it, though, didn't you."

"I like everything about you. Feeling okay?"

"I feel great." He turned on the water in the tub, waited for a decent temperature, then switched it to shower mode. Pulled back the curtain and stepped in, watched Willem join him. "I didn't think I would go twice, not so fast. You definitely liked that. Next time I'll have you in my mouth. I want to taste you. I'm so glad we did the health check."

"Jesus, me too." Willem kissed him, aware that he was half-hard again already. He tried for distraction by washing himself, then washing Richard. That particular distraction proved completely ineffective. Especially because Richard turned around and put a hand on him, going for another kiss. In a minute or two they were out of the shower, still wet, and it was Richard on his knees, Willem in his mouth, cursing and gasping and coming. "Oh my Lord."

"We'll probably be able to concentrate on food now." Richard was grinning up at him. Willem pulled him to his feet. They dried off. Richard shrugged into a Shall We Dance fight robe and handed another one to Willem.

"Oh, nice. I always wanted one of these."

Richard laughed. "I'll bet you never even thought of it till this moment."

"No, really. I saw that picture of Sam and Mateo at the last Gay Games and thought damn, that looks badass." In the kitchen, letting Richard do what he needed to do. Hanging back and watching, not really paying attention because all he wanted to think about was how wonderful this was. They took their time eating. Willem did the minimal amount of cleanup. Then it was back to bed, now simply to hold each other and kiss, and eventually to sleep.

Richard woke first. He lay there watching Willem, conscious of mild, purely opportunistic arousal. *Beautiful man in bed equals interest in sex*, he thought, amused at himself. Congratulating himself for having the idea of taking the day off. He'd made it a vacation day, telling the office administrator that he was dancing in another show and wanted to stay late at the after party. They were friendly but not the sort of friends who shared details of their love lives. Richard wondered if he could get Willem to mark him. For some reason the thought of going in with a visible sign of intimacy was highly entertaining. "What are you giggling about," Willem murmured, without opening his eyes.

"Thinking about going in to work tomorrow with a love bite on my neck."

"Did I do that?"

"Not yet."

Willem didn't say anything, only rolled over and put his mouth on Richard. It was about forty minutes before they finally got out of bed.

The day was interrupted by minor big-city annoyances like having to move Willem's car, by the necessity of regular doses of food, and by more than one shower. Otherwise they were completely wrapped up in each other, talking and kissing and making love until they were both beyond spent. Or rather, until they consciously called a halt before things could go past 'tired' to 'damaged.' They both had whisker burn, their mouths were sore from kissing, everything else was sore from everything else. "What is it about me," Richard said at some point during the evening. He wasn't keeping track of time. Willem was doing that, or had been until it was late enough that he didn't have to move his car again. They were lying in bed, face to face on their sides, with the lamps on because they wanted to see each other. Now Willem moved his head a little, as if he wasn't sure what Richard meant. "Why in the world do you love me?"

"Jesus, Richard, that's like asking why I love to dance." Richard smiled. Willem kissed him, very lightly. "From the second I saw you it was like, that's him. I don't know. Had to have you, but then we could talk, and you were smart, and it wasn't all about oh I did this gig and oh what's the next gig. Also you're beautiful." A self-deprecating look. "Stop that, you know you are. Karen showed me this vintage romance novel she found in a thrift shop. She has a few, all with covers by this guy Francis Marshall. She said, your guy looks like one of these guys, he's got that patrician thing going." He traced a fingertip over Richard's cheekbone, his nose, the curve of his mouth.

"Patrician." Richard was giggling. "You mean I could have been Fabio all this time?"

"Why not? God knows they're still publishing romance novels." The truth was he had a hard time putting this into words. His certainty that this was the man he loved was the product of so many small intersections and commonalities, parallel likes and dislikes. They found the same things funny or outrageous, they collaborated well, they seemed to be able to say anything to each other. Almost anything. Were any of those things a 'why,' or did they simply all add up to one? Willem decided to flip it around. He knew by now what an aberration their first go-around had been, never mind everything that had happened since. "Why did you say yes to a second date?"

"Because I wanted to see you again more than I wanted to hide." It was his turn to touch Willem's face, stroking a silky black eyebrow with his thumb, kissing the whisker burn on his jaw. "You're so gorgeous. You were so much fun at dinner. You were so perfect in bed. Once wasn't enough. I was surprised when you called me again."

"Too surprised to say no?"

Richard nodded. "And then you were so much fun again. We talked so long, it was too late to do anything else except kiss."

Willem remembered that kiss. Those kisses, rather, standing in the parking lot by Richard's car. Richard's hands on his body, and the soft sounds he made into Willem's mouth. "Stop that," he told his cock. Richard laughed. "Unbelievable."

"I know." Richard was remembering the third date, which started with Thai food. Feeding each other with chopsticks and fingers, completely chaotic, but every time he tried to organize himself he would look up and see Willem's beautiful face. Willem had licked his own fingers, then Richard's, and there had never been any doubt that they were going back to his room. "I was so afraid to bring you here. In retrospect I realized it couldn't have told you much about me, but we hadn't talked history at all and I didn't want you to know. I wanted you to keep thinking I was normal."

"You weren't normal. You were super-normal. You were *supernatural.* I was obsessed," Willem admitted. "I had no business going anywhere with anyone at that moment in time, but I couldn't stay away. It wasn't fair, and I'm sorry."

Richard moved away a little, enough to study Willem's face. "What? Why?"

"I was acting like this was, you know, how it was. Like I wasn't about to leave for four and a half months. I didn't even mention it on closing night. I just assumed

I could have what I wanted, up to and including another night with you before I left town." He rolled onto his back, staring at the ceiling, consciously managing his breath. "And then I was angry when you left. I should have called you."

"I didn't expect you to," Richard said softly. He put his hand on Willem's arm, needing to keep some contact. "We never talked about what came next. If there even was a next. I didn't realize how hard it was going to hit me, knowing that you were going to be gone. I only left like that because I thought I couldn't maintain. I couldn't say goodbye."

Willem turned his head. "I could have done better. We were on land two nights a week. I could have gotten my ass from Long Beach to the Westside and found you and said, hey, I wasn't ready for this to be over. Can we keep going."

"I could have found you, too," Richard pointed out. "I guess I thought if we both wanted to keep going one of us would have said something. But I basically didn't know *how* to keep going. How could we have done it? Could you have survived that contract without Jesse?"

He had to be honest. "I doubt it. That goddamned boat was a pressure cooker. There was alcohol *everywhere.* And there were meetings on board, but then my cat would have been out of its bag and I didn't know what that would do to my employability. I mean, on a lot of shows being gay is strike one, and being an alcoholic is strike two. Being a gay alcoholic might be like, you're out."

Richard nodded. "Then maybe things happened the way they needed to happen. I found out it's possible to have friends. I found out I wanted a relationship. And when we met again, I found out you didn't hate me."

"Absolute opposite of that. Come here." Richard moved, settling against Willem in the curve of his arm, resting his head on Willem's shoulder. "I love you."

"I love you too." Richard kissed his lover's chest, wrapped an arm over his ribcage, and closed his eyes. He had to trust that there would be a 'next.' Surely they hadn't made it through so much only to lose each other now.

Willem didn't leave until six forty-five Wednesday morning, barely in time to get to his car at its latest location before the rush-hour no-parking rule went into effect. "See you tonight?" he asked, because he wasn't sure.

"Jazz crew, and dinner?" Richard was much too tired to dance, but he wanted to see their friends and show off his hickey.

"You're not seriously thinking about dancing, are you? Oh, no. You're not." Willem was grinning. He kissed Richard one more time. "I love you."

"I love you too." Richard watched him go, heaved a sigh of mingled contentment and nervousness, and thought about what was going to happen in four days. He hoped the last two days, plus the last four months, would see them through it.

Chapter 18

On Sunday afternoon they walked into the hotel room Laurence and Stephanie were sharing and Willem said, “What the actual fuck.” He stared at the people assembled there. This was not what he expected.

Saturday was great; he spent all of it with his siblings doing the L.A. tourist thing, had dinner with them and Richard, then went home with his lover. Up early to get to Shall We Dance, laughing at Steph and Laurence when they showed up during the yoga class looking hungover (maybe they did some drinking after he and Richard left), and then out to brunch. Their flight back to Illinois was at oh god o’clock in the morning and he assumed they’d want to chill for a while and try to get to sleep early. Then came the invitation to come by the hotel at three because they both had some news. He assumed that meant one or the other of them was imminently reproducing. And maybe they were, frankly he was amazed they hadn’t already, but that was clearly not what was on the agenda. Rory, Dana, Sam, Mike, Andy Martin … what the *fuck*, Andy *Martin*? And his siblings, both looking nervous but resolute, who were staring not at him but at Richard. Willem turned his head, hoping his face was blank. “What’s going on.”

“I was worried about you,” Richard said. His voice was scratchy. “Very worried. I told your brother. He said he and Stephanie would come so we could talk about some things. Some things you don’t talk about. And the others are here because they’ve all either done some time in therapy like me or they’ve had some of the experiences I know you’ve had.”

"What, is someone else here a drunk?"

"You're not a drunk," Stephanie said sharply. "Willem, please sit down and talk to us. We have leaned on you for a lot of years and it's time that stopped. It's time you leaned on us a little."

He couldn't answer. Couldn't walk out, didn't want to talk, didn't know what to do but sit down. They all piled onto the king-sized bed. It should have been funny. He wanted to make a joke about a sleepover. Would have made a joke about an intervention, if it hadn't been blindingly clear that was exactly what this was. How did he know? How had Richard known how close to the edge he was? Now of all times, when so much was going right, but the ground he stood on felt like quicksand. Could he possibly have guessed how badly Willem wanted to ask for help, wanted to say 'I'm sinking'?

"I'll go first," Andy said into the silence. "Willem, I think you know I was a chorus boy for twenty years. I started at eighteen, after the usual juvenile stuff. Worked straight through, and then quit cold turkey, except for that little 'Chicago' incident. All these people know about that. Stephanie and Laurence saw the video last night."

"Great legs," Laurence said, clearly trying to lighten the mood. "That was before you stopped drinking."

"Does it show?" Willem might have sounded a little sharp. "That was a few months after I got dumped by someone who said Los Angeles was where we both belonged."

"Why did you stay?"

He turned to Andy, surprised. "Well, I had a job. Then I got the 'Chicago' thing, and it was with Robbie, and even though it was a benefit I couldn't pass up the chance to work with him. I heard all about him from Colin Firestone. We were in a show together in New York."

"I knew Colin too," Andy said. "He was a great guy." Willem watched as the older man made eye contact with everyone else. "Mr. Firestone died of cirrhosis six years ago. One of his favorite things to do was take some good-looking kid from the chorus out to bars and tell them stories about life upon the wicked stage."

Willem was annoyed. "I didn't start drinking because of him."

"Why did you start?" That was Dana.

"The same reason a lot of people start, so I didn't have to think." He didn't mean to say that.

"What did you not want to think about?" Mike, his voice even softer than usual, as if he knew what it was like to be flayed like this. Of course he did. He'd been in therapy for years after a near-fatal car crash, and again since the accident when Ray was killed. Willem didn't want to answer Mike's question. That was the whole point, he didn't want to talk about it, because he still didn't want to think about it.

"Willem." Richard's voice, almost inaudible. "Everyone here cares about you. No one is here to judge you. All we want to do is *hear* you."

"Why do you care?" Willem aimed the question at Andy.

"Because I worked with you." The impatience in that famous voice said this should be obvious. "You remind me of myself. And I've been hearing about you for going on two years, from people including my good friend Dmitri and these two nosy women right here."

“Hey,” said Rory and Dana together. Stephanie snort-laughed, then looked terrified. Dana patted her.

Laurence shifted. He wasn’t used to sitting cross-legged like this. “I’m worried that you might think the family doesn’t respect you. I can’t speak for Mom and Dad. They’re old-fashioned, and I’m sure you heard plenty of times what they wished you did with your life. You got that degree, they never understood why you didn’t go with that.”

“I did,” Willem said, annoyed all over again. “I just didn’t do it immediately.”

Sam asked, “What’s your degree in? We never talked about that. I never went to college.”

“Neither did I,” Mike said.

Andy said, “Me neither.”

“I dropped out.” Dana shrugged.

Willem looked around, confused. All these successful people, in a couple of cases famous people – even Sam had been sort of famous, during his fighting years – and *he* was the one who went to college. “Maybe it was a complete waste of time. Kinesiology.”

“Obviously not a complete waste of time,” Rory said, irritated. “Since you are now a fitness professional. After twenty years in one of the most difficult, most competitive professions known to humankind. Now, *my* college degree, in English for fuck’s sake, was a complete waste of time.”

“Not complete.” There was a trace of a smile in Richard’s voice now. “It helped you get in at the law firm, and I got to know you.”

“Good point. But we’re getting sidetracked, because this is supposed to be about you.” Rory stared at Willem.

"I'd rather talk about all of you." He let himself fall over backward, staring at the ceiling. Richard touched his chest, tentatively. Willem took his hand. "I'm not mad. I'm … freaked out. I don't know where to start. I don't want to talk about when, or how, or why."

"Tell us why you were willing to keep me and Steph from flunking out of math instead of saying figure it out yourselves, you little boneheads," Laurence suggested.

"Well, Dad sucked at it, and Mom was the most impatient teacher in the world, and I didn't mind." That wasn't the whole truth. He might as well say everything; clearly they weren't letting him out of here until he did. "I felt like it gave me some value. Mom and Dad didn't exactly thank me, but you guys did."

"You didn't *mind.*" Stephanie sounded incredulous. "You lost sleep over it. I know you did. You stayed up with me that time, I was having such an awful time with long division, I was *crying*. You stayed up until I finally got it. Mom and Dad had been in bed for an hour. You carried me to my room."

His brother said, "You were a better parent than they were, half the time." Willem blinked hard, swallowed, forced a breath through the tightness in his throat. Laurence said slowly, as if he'd only now remembered, "But you were already drinking then."

"Jesus! How old were you?" That was Andy.

"Long division? Steph was eight. I was thirteen. I started drinking when I was nine." It felt like all the air got sucked out of the room for a second. Everyone was so appalled, it was a physical sensation. Richard's hand closed convulsively on his. Willem was lightheaded with horror and relief. It would all come out now, it had to.

"Because you didn't want to think," Sam said after a long moment. "Willem, what happened to you?"

"Oh my *God.*" Laurence again. "Our grandfather died when I was sixteen. Willem was eighteen. He was already living in Chicago and he didn't come home for the funeral because he was in a show. Our mother found, oh *Jesus*."

"She found pictures." Stephanie sounded like she couldn't breathe, or like she was about to vomit. "Pictures of boys. *Willem*."

"That was why. That was why you never let me be in a room alone with him."

"I hit him once," Willem said, dimly aware that all of them were touching him, and that tears were leaking from under his eyelids. "When he said he loved you. I was eleven. I said, touch him and I will burn your house down around you. He laughed at me. He thought I was jealous."

Richard's whole body was shaking. "How long?"

"Eight to twelve. Then I got too tall."

"You were away that summer," Stephanie said, voice trembling. "At theater camp. You grew so much while you were gone."

Willem kept his eyes closed, willing himself not to picture it. Not to remember that day when his grandfather looked at him with disappointment, as if Willem had failed him somehow, and he'd thought *I won*. He'd made it through, and no one knew, and his brother was still safe. Laurence went to Canada that summer, with a friend's family. It was the only reason Willem agreed to go away. And Willem had grown strong enough that if the old man tried anything he could kill him. He wanted to.

Laurence was crying. "You kept me safe. Oh God, did they know? Did Mom and Dad know? Did they let that happen to you?"

"I don't think they knew. He knew it was wrong. He was sly. It was a year before I really understood, and then all I could think was, it's been a year, no one has even noticed, no one will believe me. And I watched Dad make himself a drink after work, and saw how it helped him relax, and I thought, maybe that will help me too."

Everyone was silent for a minute. Maybe they couldn't think of anything to say. Richard certainly couldn't. And he couldn't imagine how Willem had even survived, much less achieved what he had. After another minute he said that. Then he added, "What happened this year? You've done so spectacularly with your business. You're so wonderful with me. Did something about my bullshit take you back? Was I the problem?" He didn't want to make this about him, but he'd been afraid of it ever since he realized there *was* a problem.

"You could not possibly be a problem. Nothing about you is a problem." Willem sat up, wiped his face, and concentrated on Richard as if he were the only other person in the room. "I couldn't believe it was working. I've felt so damaged, and filthy, and disgusting for so long. I felt like such a fraud. Like any minute, everyone in the world was going to figure out how worthless I was. I felt like I didn't deserve you."

Richard closed his eyes, took a steadying breath, then opened his eyes again. He put on his best Agent Smith look and said, "I will be the judge of that." That almost got a laugh, he was sure of it. They were so close together, and even with all those other people in the room he was going to do this. "'You are the best thing that ever happened to me.'"

He sang it, and his ruined voice sounded so perfect that Willem went to pieces. When he finally stopped crying, his head was on Richard's lap. That narrow body was curved protectively over him. His face hurt, his throat hurt, and he didn't want to think about how he must look. He kept his eyes closed while his breath slowly settled and the tremor subsided. Richard stroked back his hair and said something to someone. Then there was a handful of tissue. Willem blew his nose. Someone handed him a damp washcloth to cool his face. He eventually sat up. Everyone was gone except his siblings and Richard. He didn't know what to say.

"Mr. Martin left his card," Stephanie said. She was sitting on the room's sleeper sofa now, pale and red-eyed. "He said you should call him to talk about second and third acts." Willem nodded.

Laurence was leaning against the wall. He looked almost as bad as Willem felt. "I called our parents and Lynette. Steph called Bobby and Dr. Rogers. We're staying another day."

"What did you tell them?" His voice didn't even sound like his own.

"We didn't tell anybody anything, except that we had a family emergency. I'll talk to Mom and Dad face to face."

Richard's hand was on Willem's back. "And you'll take another day off," he said softly but firmly. Willem nodded again. "I'm not going to ask if you feel better. But do you feel like you can go on? Go forward?"

"Yes. Thank you." Willem heaved a sigh. "What time is it? It feels like midnight."

Stephanie looked at her phone. "Not even six o'clock. Full day. Reminds me of the time a lady came in for a checkup and turned out to be six centimeters dilated."

Willem appreciated the attempt at lightness. "Reminds me of the time a bunch of us showed up for rehearsal and found out the director and choreographer got fired and we had to start over." He stirred. "Is there some water?"

Laurence handed him a bottle from the mini bar. "Before we go back to our usual mode, I want to say one thing. Stephanie and I always idolized you. You were our rock. You showed us the horizon. We would not be who we are without you. So for fuck's sake, talk about this shit until it doesn't tear you apart anymore. We need you." His voice went wrong again and he sniffed, swallowed, wiped his eyes.

Willem did the same. "Deal." He turned his head, made eye contact with Richard. "I'll make a deal with you, too." Richard's eyebrows went up inquiringly. "I'll move in with you if you'll marry me." He didn't even wait for the 'yes' before going in for a kiss. He heard it a minute later, when they were holding each other. "I love you," he said into Richard's hair.

"I love you too. We are going to be okay." Richard sat back a little, holding Willem's face between his hands. Searching his eyes. "Yes?"

"Yes." Willem kissed him one more time. "I need to move." Richard smiled. They both turned to look at Stephanie and Laurence, collected nods of agreement, and slid off the bed.

An hour later, they were all limbered up and relaxed after a slow amble through Beverly Hills. They went to Ocean Prime for dinner and talked about what was happening in their work lives. It wasn't until they were ambling back down Wilshire Boulevard to the hotel that Stephanie said, "So about this proposal." Willem made a sound approximating 'oh Lord.' "Can we tell Mom and Dad about that? Is there a plan?"

"There is no plan." Richard was holding one of Willem's hands. He caught hold of his sister with the other. "I knew I wanted to ask him but it was on this long list of things I was afraid to do."

"Why were you afraid?" Richard gave him a sideways look. "Did I fail to communicate something?"

"No," Willem said patiently. "But we just went to bed five minutes ago and, you know."

Stephanie was laughing. Laurence said, "Uh, TMI. Except wait, what? Were you not this whole time?"

"We were not," Richard answered. "Our first round didn't end well and we agreed not to rush it again. Though personally I think we could have accelerated things just a little." He glanced sideways again and laughed. Willem was blushing.

It wasn't so funny when they were alone. The humor they'd found to get them through the evening all fled when they were at Richard's apartment washing up, and then going to bed. Willem let Richard be the strong one, holding him, kissing him softly, saying, "What do you need, sweetheart. What can I do."

Willem sighed against his chest. He was exhausted, and his throat still hurt, and he wanted sex because that would help him forget, but the whole point was that he couldn't. "I never mixed it up, you know."

Richard thought about this for a minute. "You mean sex? What he did to you and what you did by choice?"

"Yeah. What he did was wrong, and foul, and it fucked me up. But he didn't actually fuck me."

"Well, thank God for that."

Willem almost laughed. "Yeah. I don't want to tell you. I don't want you to picture it."

"You don't have to tell me anything. Someday you should tell someone, though." Willem hated the thought of verbalizing it. It seemed as though those mental pictures would somehow become more concrete if he verbalized. Maybe that came across in his silence now. Richard kissed him again. Willem clung to him, pressing close. They kissed until they were both breathless, Richard half on top of Willem and urgent against him. He lifted his head and started to move down Willem's body.

"No, stay. Keep kissing me. Up a little." Willem got a hand in between them. Richard lifted his body slightly, gasping into Willem's mouth as that hand closed around him. He pushed into it with a hungry sound, head going back, neck arching. "Yes. Richard. I love you. Come for me." His other hand brought Richard's mouth back to his. He barely moved then, because Richard was moving against him and it was enough, it was perfect, "Oh *God*," he said into that open mouth as the climax took him. Richard felt the pulse, the wetness, and made a harsh sound. His body jerked. He was propped on his hands, each breath slightly vocal, his mouth barely touching Willem's. Moving fast in that wet hand. "Come on baby. Now. Yes, fucking hell, *now*."

Richard bucked against him, coming hard. "Jesus!" A soft, satisfied laugh, then Willem let him go. Wrapped both arms around him and pulled him down. After a minute Richard said, "We'll get stuck together."

"Good."

"I love you."

"I love you too."

Chapter 19

April 2018

Willem heard from either his brother or his sister every day for a while. He wanted to resent it – he was a grown man, he had Richard checking in all the time, not to mention Karen, not to mention his landlady – but it was impossible. Even though, somewhere in that damaged part of his brain, the fear kept bubbling up, it couldn't get past the wall of love. All that love saying yes, you're worthy. Yes, you're special. Yes, you matter. Perhaps most importantly: yes, we need you.

The days at work went by in their orderly way. Yoga, dance, the gym; classes and private lessons and coaching. People noticed something different. He'd always done such a good job of hiding his troubles. It was still habitual, and he wouldn't tell a client such personal things anyway, but he could tell them he was engaged. That news may or may not have pleased everyone; Willem didn't really care. Saying it out loud always launched a rocket of happiness.

Then, thirteen days after the intervention, he got a letter. An actual letter, through the actual mail, because his parents were old-fashioned. He was almost afraid to open it. Laurence had assured him that the conversation happened, that their parents were appalled, that – he said – they were praying about it. That particular news didn't reassure Willem. The church had never provided him with meaningful guidance, let alone protection, and the idea of some immanent spirit having the ability (or motivation) to intervene in the individual lives of humans seemed laughable. He kept that skepticism to himself at meetings.

He knew he had to read the letter. If there was something in it that he needed to cope with, he didn't want to do that in front of Richard. Even though Richard loved him no matter what, or maybe because of that. There was only so much coping one person should be asked to do. After some dithering, he checked his schedule and sent a text: *Hi gorgeous I'm going to a meeting after my last client, will come over after. Hope you had a good day. Love you XOX*

As usual on a Saturday, a reply came back fast: *Thanks for letting me know. Will you be hungry when you get here? Love you XOX*

Good chance of that. Can't wait to kiss you

LOL I said hungry not horny but that works too. See you later sweetheart XOX

All the XOX. Willem put the phone away and went back to work, resolutely not thinking past the next few clients.

Eventually, of course, he couldn't put it off any longer. He found a parking space close enough to the meeting, an hour before it was due to begin. Had a drink of water from his travel bottle, pushed his seat back so he could stretch his legs, and opened the letter.

> Dear Willem, our dear son,
>
> We are so very sorry. We failed you. It has taken this long for us to write only because we had to start so many times. We wanted to call but we weren't sure you would want us to. Laurence told us how you have struggled to speak of what happened, and we are so sorry. We feel that we made it impossible for you to speak. It must have been our fault. You were always the open one, the loving one. We both failed at that, with Laurence

and Stephanie too. We have all been talking together, crying together. Regretting together.

How could we not have known? How could we not have guessed, especially after Tata died and we found those pictures, when we knew he spent so much time with you. You seemed different at nine but we thought it was only because you were growing and changing. We had troubles, such trivial troubles, with our work or with money or with being parents. We failed. We did not ask questions, not the right questions. We did not give you a way to speak to us. We let you lead your brother and sister, and you did it so well. You protected Laurence and we failed to protect you. You were so strong. You knew what you wanted, it seemed, and you had such talent we couldn't say no even though we were afraid it would make your life so difficult.

The stage was the only place you could be yourself. You told us that when you were sixteen. We remembered that when you were eighteen and went to Chicago, and when you went to New York. We were so afraid for you then. But you were so strong, and you never asked for help, and you never confessed even to loneliness. You must have been so lonely. We are so very, very sorry.

We do not know how, or whether, you will want to go on with us. We hope you can forgive us. We pray for that. We admire you so much. We are so proud of you. And we are so happy for you, that you and Richard will be married, that you have someone who loves you as you deserve. We hope you will bring him to meet us when you are ready. He will be welcome here. We love you.

Mom & Dad

Willem leaned back in the seat, tipped his head up, and didn't even try to stop the tears. It was a good thing he read this before going home. Or going to Richard, which meant the same thing. A good thing there was a meeting only a few steps and a few minutes away. The letter meant so much, but he was so angry. Furiously, screamingly angry, and there was no point to it. He couldn't say anything that would make his parents feel worse. That penitent letter was like nothing he'd ever seen, like no words they had ever spoken. He couldn't rage at the old man, dead almost twenty years. All he could do was feel it, acknowledge it, accept it, and let it go. *This is a thing you cannot change.* After a while he wiped his face, drank some more water, and went to the meeting.

At first he only listened. He still wasn't sure he wanted to talk about this. More accurately, he was sure he didn't want to talk about it. But he'd promised to, and he needed to, and if he didn't talk about it he was wasting his time here. So when there came a pause, and the leader looked around the circle, he sat forward. That small movement gathered everyone's attention, perhaps because he'd been so utterly still up to now.

"My name is Willem," he said, "and I'm an alcoholic. I've been sober for over nine years. I started drinking when I was nine years old." He ignored the rustle of reaction. "That was a year after my grandfather started molesting me." Sounds of shock and revulsion. Willem kept his gaze steady, directed at the floor in the middle of the circle. "I never told anyone until this year. I don't want to talk about it. But it was screwing me up. I'm in a relationship. I'm in love, we're engaged. I don't – I didn't believe I deserved that." Words coming in a flood. "I was fighting that, because he loves me with all he has, and he is not a guy who loves or trusts easily. He trusted me, and I trust him. He saw me struggling. He got me help. And this thing I can't talk about is why I used to drink, so I have to talk about it, because I want to deserve him and I want us to have forever. We deserve that." Saying it out loud felt good. Almost good enough to stitch together the hole in his gut. He breathed slowly, consciously, listening to the absolute silence in the room. After a minute he lifted his gaze and looked around. "That's all I have today. I don't want a drink. I want to go home."

The leader's face was pale and he looked shaken. "Thank you, Willem. Anyone else?" A chorus of No and Not today. "Okay. Let's repeat the twelve steps." They did that, and they recited the serenity prayer, and then they all stood up to go. Willem didn't want to chat. He moved out of there fast, trying not to feel exposed and judged and weak. The first two might be true, the third was not. He knew it wasn't. He wouldn't be alive if he were weak.

In his car, buckled up and ready to go, he checked in with himself. He didn't feel better, necessarily, but he didn't feel worse. Before putting the car in gear he pulled out his phone and sent a text: *Hi sweetheart starting over now, ETA 15 min. Love you.* Then another: *Hi Mom, Hi Dad, thanks for your letter. I'll be in touch soon about a visit. I love you.* He sent it off, knowing he wasn't quite to 'I forgive you' yet, but feeling like it might be possible someday. Then he put the phone away again, checked for traffic, and pulled out of the parking space.

Richard looked up from the couch as the door opened, reached for the remote, and paused the DVD he had playing. "Are you all right, honey?" He was getting to his feet as he spoke. Willem didn't answer immediately, only dropped his gear bag in the corner and waited for the incoming hug. He didn't seem to want to let go. Richard held on. "What happened?"

After a minute Willem eased back, enough for a kiss, and said, "I love you."

"I love you too. What is it?"

"I got a letter from my parents. I talked about … stuff, at the meeting."

"What do you need, sweetheart."

Willem kissed him again. "Only you. It's a good letter. Do you want to read it?"

He wouldn't have offered if he didn't want Richard to see it. He nodded, studying that beloved face. "You need to eat something."

"Did you?"

Richard made an impatient noise, half-amused. "Yes. Come on." He took Willem into the kitchen. They put together a generous snack for Willem and a small one for Richard, then went to the living room. "Eat first. Then I'll read the thing." He didn't watch Willem eat, knowing all too well how annoying that could be. Instead he paid attention to his own food. Another small victory over the disorder. When they both sat back, he could tell Willem was more relaxed. It was a shame he couldn't just leave this alone. An open door must be walked through, no matter what monsters were on the other side. "I was wondering if they would get in touch. I was hoping they would." *It was their job.*

"I think it was hard for them." Willem stood up, collected their plates, and took those back to the kitchen. He dug the letter out of his bag before returning, handing it to Richard without a word.

Richard waited until Willem sat down again, then wriggled around until he'd maneuvered the other man into the corner of the couch (he was smiling by that point) so Richard could lean back against his chest. Willem wrapped an arm around his waist and kissed the side of his face. Only then did Richard pull the letter out of the envelope and start to read. When he finished, he folded it again, slid it back into the envelope, and dropped it on the coffee table. "That is a good letter."

"No excuses."

"Did they ever say that before? That they admire you, or that they're proud of you?"

Willem thought back. "I can't remember. I know they told me I'd done well, sometimes. Congratulated me. It always seemed … conditional."

"Maybe because they were afraid," Richard suggested. "Afraid to encourage you, because they thought what you were doing was risky." Willem made a noncommittal sound. "Yes, I know it's an unsatisfactory and possibly overgenerous interpretation." Now an amused sound. "What really annoys me, on the career side, is they never seemed to recognize what an amazing success you were."

"What a what?"

Richard twisted around to see the expression that went with that astounded tone of voice. "Willem van der Meer. Do you seriously not think you were a success? Do we need to put every show you've done, every credit, up on the wall? Because I will do that."

Willem was half-laughing, half-embarrassed. "I know I had a lot of jobs. I guess it never felt like success because," he pondered for a few seconds, "maybe because I never had starring roles. I was never the lead." It felt like a revelation. "Is that one of those set-yourself-up-to-fail things, or what?"

"Willem. What the hell do you even mean." Richard squirmed around to fully face him.

"I didn't *audition* for the leads! I was always, well, it's not an Asian role, or I'm too young, or I'm too old, or for fuck's fucking sake. I can't believe I did that to myself."

"I can't either. Except I can. There were times when my thing was telling me the only reason I wasn't working was because I was too big. And that was long after I decided to quit. I *chose* to quit. I was like, shut up you asshole." Willem snorted. Richard smiled a little, touching his lover's face. "All the time. Shut up shut up shut up. Sometimes I could dance my way out of it."

"Do you still get that?" Willem's voice was soft.

"Sometimes. It tries everything. I've got better tools now. I've got weapons."

I need better tools, Willem thought. *I need weapons*. "I think I had armor. But that's not the same, is it? All that shit was still out there bashing away at me."

"I wish I could tell you it will go away." Richard moved. Willem moved. In a few seconds they were lying down together, holding each other close. Richard petted Willem's hair. "Some days the fight is harder than others. You know that as well as anyone. But I will always, always be here. To help, or to listen, or just to keep you company. You are not in this alone anymore."

"Same. All of that. You and me against the assholes." Willem felt Richard's laugh, a silent vibration against his body and a puff of breath against his neck. He turned his head for a kiss. "I love you so much." Another, deeper, more intentional kiss.

"Mmm. Show me how much."

Richard went into his next appointment with Dr. Simon with a lot to say. "I did it," he said as soon as the therapist sat down. "Staged an intervention." Dr. Simon stared at him over the top of his reading glasses, tapping his pen against his notepad. Richard almost smiled at how stagily shrinkish he looked. "It worked."

A visible intake of breath, and a ghost of a smile. "In what sense?"

"In the sense that Willem told us when his problem started, and how, and why. The why is pretty horrible. Told us why he'd been spiraling lately, even though things have been going so well. His brother and sister were here and they all said some important things. They really love him."

"That's good. Who else was there?"

"My two best girl friends, one of whom has a shrink she's been seeing for years. One of my best guy friends – the fashionista – and a dance friend who's been through a lot of therapy, and a TV star we know who's basically an older version of Willem. He was a Broadway dancer too, and he's done therapy. Everybody was like, we're not here to judge you. We're here to listen. Please talk to us. And maybe he was only waiting for permission. He let it all out."

"And it was helpful?"

"I think it really was. All that awful tension is gone. It's like he was afraid if he ever said these things something terrible would happen. But he said them, and nothing bad happened. He's sleeping better. He's staying at my place almost every night." Richard could tell the counselor wanted to ask about that. "I already told him he should move in with me. He said he would, if I would marry him."

Dr. Simon dropped his pen, sat back, flung up both hands, and said, "Please tell me you said yes." Richard laughed. The shrink groped under his chair for his pen, then sat up again, looking very pleased. "So how about you."

"I am doing well. I feel good. We have a routine, and you know I do better with a routine. He's still, I want to say alert. He can tell when it's not a good day, and he has ways of helping me do better. He makes it easier for me to do better. We're not preparing a new dance right now but we're talking about trying out for a show once the notice goes up."

"That's excellent. The same kind of thing?"

"No, it would be a much bigger thing. Like the thing he was doing when we met. A full program, performed three times. Probably three months of rehearsals."

"Good gracious. That's ambitious."

Richard nodded. "I asked my doctor if I'm healthy enough. She looked at me like she didn't know why I was asking. I said, you know I have this condition. She said Richard, you're managing it. If this is something you want to do, but you feel like you have some limitations, just be honest with yourself and with the people you're working with. Don't get competitive, and you'll be fine." He observed the therapist's 'sounds reasonable' expression. "You agree?"

Dr. Simon tapped his pen again. "I saw that number you did in February."

"Oh, you did?" Richard wasn't sure if he should be delighted or nervous. "What did you think?"

"I was, frankly, astonished. The way you've always talked about dancing, I did not imagine anything like that."

"I wouldn't have myself, before Willem. We did those three dances, and each one was different, and we both learned so much. That one," he paused for a second, "it was therapy. For both of us. We knew it even while we were making it. All of our friends say, we had no idea. And we always say, we didn't either."

Dr. Simon made a note, then simply sat and studied Richard for a minute. "You have made remarkable progress in the past year and a half. What I'm seeing is a much more well-rounded person. Would you agree?"

"Oh, definitely. Even going out dancing with Sam and Mateo felt like such a big thing at first, or going out to dinner. Doing the jazz class. Going out to see dance things, by myself. I know the feeling that everyone is watching me is part of the neurosis. Part of the disorder. So I go out, to the movie theater to see a Bolshoi livestream or something like that, and I make a point of centering myself. I look around at who else is there. Nobody's ever paying attention to me. Sometimes someone will notice me noticing them."

"What happens then?"

"Then, instead of panicking and looking away, I smile. And one hundred percent of the time, they smile back. It's bizarre." Dr. Simon laughed. Richard almost laughed too. "I have such a full life now. So many friends. When we get married, I'd like to bring Willem in so we could talk to you together."

"Oh, so it's *when.* Sure. I think that would be a good thing."

Richard was faintly smiling now. “You’re going to be looking to see if he’s doing some Svengali number on me, aren’t you.”

“Hey. Whatever he’s doing, it’s clearly benign. At least.” Dr. Simon’s phone alarm went off. “I would like to say congratulations, Mr. Hollister. For dealing with a difficult problem exceptionally well, and on your engagement. I look forward to seeing what you do next.”

“Thank you. So do I.”

Chapter 20

When it came right down to it, neither of them had ever seriously thought about getting married. At dinner with Rory, Dana, Sam, and Mateo, having decided that the best source of inspiration might be their own recently-married friends, Richard confessed, "It never occurred to me that was a thing that could happen. I mean, before last year I hadn't even *been* to a wedding since right after college. We thought yours was beautiful," he added, looking at Dana.

"But neither of us is really a church person, and our families aren't going to be here." Willem caught Spike's fluffy tail before it could swoosh into his plate.

"Why not?" Mateo gave them both a sharp look.

Willem gave him one back. "They're not invited." He passed the cat to his fiancé.

Richard settled Spike down and said, "It was great to meet Stephanie and Laurence but they can't come out here again so soon, and we don't want to go there. Not in the immediate future, anyway. Your wedding was nice too." He directed that to Sam.

"It got a little silly," Rory said grumpily. The celebrant for Sam and Mateo, she'd found herself being shamelessly pressured into accepting Dana's long-standing proposal. "I mean, the result was satisfactory."

Dana leaned in and nudged her wife, smiling fondly. "Knucklehead."

Rory nudged back. "Whatever. Anyway, the yard is available to you and even if you don't want to do it here I'd be happy to do your ceremony. Do you want to invite people? I mean, last year's things were all kind of big."

Richard and Willem gazed at each other for a moment. "I think I'd like it really small," Willem said. "Would that be okay with you?"

"That's fine. Do you want to do it here?" The yard was nice, but if they weren't inviting people they needed some pictures. Richard wasn't sure the yard was the ideal venue. Hard to control. Maybe something a little more structured would be better.

Maybe Rory read his mind. "You know, when Vicky and Sharon got married we did it guerrilla-style at Urban Light. Only eight people there even knew what we were doing."

Sam nodded. "Vicky loves to tell that story."

Richard really liked the idea. "That sounds great. All of you and Karen?" He could tell Willem was in favor too. They wouldn't even have to drive anywhere; they could walk over from the apartment. "We could have dinner at Spare Tire after."

"I might jump on a streetlamp like Gene Kelly."

"I'm counting on it." They grinned at each other. Willem leaned in for a kiss. Richard took his hand off the cat and put it on his fiancé's thigh. "Oh my God, we're getting *married*. What a *trip*." They managed a hug, ignoring a hissed complaint from Spike. "When?"

They got their phones out, found a date that worked for all six of them, and Willem called Karen. "Do you have a minute? Super fast, I promise. Are you free around seven on this date in May? A thing and dinner. Richard and I are getting married." He had to wait a minute for the excitement on the other end to abate, holding eye contact with Richard. "At Urban Light. Our friend Rory is doing it. Yes, that Rory, from the 'Bang Bang' routine. She's ordained by the Universal Life Church. I mean yeah, the spaghetti monster thing would be good, but you go with what you got."

"They can't officiate," Rory said, "or that would've been the one." Mateo and Dana snickered.

Willem was smiling at whatever Karen was saying. "So we'll see you there, and I'll see you before then. Thanks sweetie. Oh my God yes, I'm so excited. Love you too." He disconnected. "How long does it take to get a license?"

"About twenty minutes if you go at the right time." Mateo paused for a swallow of wine. "Or all day, if you do like we did and go straight home to fool around."

Richard laughed. "I can't imagine I'm going to be worth a damn at work after that."

"Then I guess it's another vacation day." Willem took a second to check in with himself and see if this was cause for anxiety, decided it truly wasn't, and kissed Richard again. They kissed some more when they got in the car to go home, and more after parking. They kissed while walking to the apartment, and in the elevator going upstairs. Once in the bedroom, they lay down together and simply held each other. "This is not where I imagined being, a year ago," Willem said after a while. Then, in case Richard was wondering what he meant, he added, "Engaged to you. In love with you. In your bed. In your arms."

"You never imagined this?"

"Oh, I imagined *some* of it." They both laughed softly. "But I could only imagine variations on what I remembered, you know? That was enough to get me through some bad nights. This is all so much more."

"It is kind of incredibly much more. I love you." Richard laid a hand on Willem's face, stroking up over his cheekbone and into his hair. "This is enough to get us through anything, isn't it?"

"It has to be. I love you. I think I've loved you since that first day, I just didn't know what it was."

"I knew what it was." Richard's tone was rueful. "I didn't want to believe it. Because if we couldn't come back to each other, I didn't know how to get over you. I did try."

"I'm glad it didn't work." Another quiet moment, then: "I talk about you at meetings. About how we met and kind of messed up, but came back and tried again. I said once, it seems as though being in love is like being sober, something you have to be conscious about every day."

Richard blinked, swallowed, and took a breath. "That's a nice way to think of it. Maybe that's why you're good at it."

Willem smiled. "Because I've had so much practice? Maybe so." One more kiss. "Let's get ready for bed."

Willem was surprised to find Dmitri at Shall We Dance when they arrived. The boss dropped in occasionally to co-lead the Cardio Latin class, but most Sundays were a day off for him. This time he seemed to be there for a specific purpose, which was to say, "You do not call Andy yet."

Willem felt as guilty as if he'd been caught breaking into a car. "Uh, no. I will, I promise."

"Soon. He is busy."

"Yes sir. I mean okay." He turned toward Richard and made a silent, big-eyed 'what the fuck' face. Richard was stifling laughter. "Go stretch, honey."

"Yes sir," Richard murmured, and went to take off his shoes. He watched Willem prepare for the yoga class, putting on that character to greet the incoming students. He wondered sometimes if his lover was aware he did that, or if it was an instinctive thing. Then he thought about Dmitri, coming in on his day off to remind Willem about that invitation. He knew Andy really was busy, not only with wrapping up another season on 'L.A. Vice' but with pre-production for a movie. Richard and Willem had signed up for a three-hour Argentine tango boot camp in May, from which dance extras for the movie would be cast. Richard had a good grounding in Argentine tango already, from the teacher training. Willem claimed he knew nothing. They were both excited about doing the boot camp, and the chance to be in a movie together.

Richard didn't fully participate in the yoga class that day. He was feeling lazy. They'd spent an enjoyable two hours at Mandy's studio the night before. Willem was coaching a student of hers who had a Broadway-style routine going into the April showcase at Chrome. Richard contributed a few character notes, ran the video camera and the music, and thought about their wedding plans. Then they went home and had dinner while talking about their wedding plans. After that, lovemaking, and again this morning. He was pleasantly exhausted, and somehow not at all surprised when Dmitri joined him on the floor and said, "I lead Cardio Latin today. You are tired."

The students always loved it when Dmitri was there. So Richard didn't argue, only said, "Yes sir." Dmitri gave him an amused glance. He didn't seem at all tired himself, though maybe he should have; there was a love bite on his neck. Richard looked away so he wouldn't laugh. Dmitri was never obvious and always discreet, but since he retired from competition the passionate nature of his marriage had become more evident. Richard loved the thought of still feeling this way in thirty years.

The Sunday classes were full these days. Like a lot of fitness things (especially low-cost things), they tended to be packed in January and then taper off. But Willem was succeeding here just as he was everywhere else. Halfway through the Tone and Tune class, there was really no space for anyone else to join. A few people poked their heads in and made disappointed faces. Richard sidled down the wall to speak with them. They said they'd get there earlier next time. After Willem wound up the session, he came to join Richard and said, "I wasn't expecting it to stay full."

"You haven't been reading the comments." Richard leaned over for a kiss. "Dmitri's going to run my class. Are you going to dance?"

What Willem really wanted to do was go back home, and back to bed, with Richard. He was insatiable these days, and Richard was no good at saying No. So instead, he said, "Yeah, I think I will. I'm starting to get the hang of jive."

"We'll turn you into a ballroom dancer yet." They were standing close together. Richard could feel Willem's body heat. Thirty years with this man was not going to be enough. "Go get some water before he starts."

"Yes sir." Willem kissed him again, started to turn away, then stepped back and wrapped an arm around Richard's neck, pulling him in for another, longer, deeper kiss. "God I love you."

"I love you too." Richard was a little breathless, and more than a little turned on. He went into the office to settle himself down by updating the attendance logs. Halfway into Dmitri's cha-cha section he emerged again, watching the class assimilate the short combination and dance it through a bunch of times. Everyone was smiling. It was always like that, even when Richard was leading the class, but everyone here today was charged up because of Dmitri.

Part of the appeal was, of course, that he was The Boss and everyone knew it. Even a newcomer couldn't miss it, with the big framed photos of Dmitri and Michelle during their second World Championship campaign. Another part of it was his natural gravitas, which made people feel they were doing something consequential even though it was only a casual Sunday-morning class.

A big part of it, Richard knew, was the voice. Dmitri's wasn't stage-trained, or otherwise remarkable. It was a calm, steady baritone, with an accent most people found attractive. He rarely had to repeat himself. Richard did, frequently, because as a class progressed and people relaxed (or started having fun) they forgot he couldn't be louder. His vocal technique was well-developed, but the instrument itself couldn't overcome chatter. It was probably the most fatiguing thing about leading group classes. There was no training that could make up for that deficit.

His mother had, for years, been trying to convince him to have surgery. As far as he could tell from reading about the possibilities, he was nearly as likely to come away with more damage as with improvement. The odds weren't good enough to risk it. His clerks and his friends didn't care if he didn't sound like someone who'd once been on Broadway. Willem didn't either. He said the line from that song was the most beautiful thing he'd ever heard.

As usual, thinking of Willem resulted in looking at Willem, who as usual was gazing back at him as if there'd been some kind of signal. Richard smiled, strongly tempted to join for the last third of the class. Instead, to conserve his energy, he went to a chair and sat down to watch.

Richard got another reminder of (or lesson in) what was possible the following Sunday. After the community classes and brunch, they went to the renovated duplex called the Faux Chateau. Out in the backyard in the sun, with snacks, beverages, a friendly blonde dog, movie star Victor Garcia, and his husband Andy. They were so much in love it was like a neon sign. The conversation was purely social for a while, which gave Willem and Richard both a feeling something like vertigo, but before long Andy suggested they go up to his home studio to talk. "Mr. Garcia will be napping in approximately two minutes," he said.

"Yes I will." Victor stretched luxuriously on his lounger. "Give me one more of those cookies before you take them away."

Andy put a cookie in his hand, snapped the lid on the container, leaned down for a kiss and to say, "See you later, catnip," then led the way across the yard. His home studio was above the four-car garage off the alley. Richard had been there a few times, for not-so-intimate things, mostly related to the Cabaret.

Willem had been there only once before, for Andy's most recent photography show, 'The Male Animal.' Some of those pictures were still on the wall. "You sold all the others?"

"No, gave them to the subjects. I'm selling prints through the online store. The other guys will pick theirs up eventually."

“Where’s yours?” Richard would have thought the image of nearly-nude Andy in a swan-like pose would stay in place. It was the kind of picture anyone would want to have, at any age, much less at fifty-plus. “Did you put it in the house?”

Andy looked mildly embarrassed. “Victor wanted it in there, yeah. We hung it in the guest room.” He pointed to the two folding chairs next to his task chair. “No luxury up here, sorry. I’m really not sure if you want my opinions or advice, Willem, but since we have a pretty chunky piece of common experience they are available to you.”

Willem took a seat. “I’d like to hear from you. Last month things went a different direction.”

“They went where they needed to go. What I meant to get to was the question of professional input. I know Richard has a shrink.”

Richard nodded. “Dr. Simon. He’s helped me a lot.” He pulled the third chair close to Willem and sat down.

“Finding a good fit isn’t all that easy. I’ve seen various people at various times and some of them were not all that helpful.” Andy shrugged. “But they listened, which is the main thing, and telling them stuff meant I didn’t have to either internalize it or spew it at someone inappropriate.”

Willem was still back at ‘various people.’ “When were you in therapy?”

“A bunch of times. I don’t have an ongoing issue that I wanted help dealing with. For me it’s kind of like getting my teeth cleaned, part of regular maintenance. The first time was about, Jesus, thirty years ago. It was when I was in New York, and people were dying. In the Eighties,” he clarified. “AIDS went through Broadway like a fucking forest fire. It's one thing to lose an old person. It's different when it's someone ten years older than you, or five. I hadn't been there long enough to get really close to anybody but, you know. A show experience can get intimate fast."

"Yeah." Willem was processing. By the time he went to New York, the worst of the plague was over.

"Anyway. There was a bad breakup. I saw someone after that. Then there was a time when someone I cared about wanted something I couldn't agree to. A good breakup, in the big picture, but a hard one. There was the time I knew I had to stop." They all knew he meant 'stop dancing.'

"You were still getting cast."

"Sure, but at thirty-seven – that's how old I was when I went out on my last tour – I wasn't bouncing back. I could still lay it out on the stage, but I was paying for it. It was only a matter of time before I got injured. And I'd been getting *not* cast since a few years before. But honestly, I'd started to want a home. You were trying to keep a home base, weren't you?"

Willem nodded. "It wasn't everything, but it was better than nothing. I did some tours and it was really hard to stay sober. Trying to find a meeting. Trying not to annoy the rest of the cast. I mean, everyone drinks."

"Oh, I know. I was a holy terror on tour. I still drink a lot, probably more than I should, because I like it. I've never felt like I was possibly getting dependent except when we were renovating this place. Victor and I lived in here, this studio, before the main house was finished. Lots of junk food, and alcohol substituted for real food, because there's no real kitchen. Almost six months of awful hours thanks to that fucking TV show." He made a sound best described as a growl.

Richard tried not to laugh. "Mateo said, way back, if I ever asked you about it you would say you hate that fucking show."

"I totally do. It's been good to us and especially to Victor, so I suck it up. Which brings us to what's next, Mr. van der Meer."

Willem looked startled. "What's next?"

"Well, clearly you have a gift as an instructor. If you love it there's no reason not to keep doing that for the next twenty or thirty years. But you have other options."

Willem thought he meant acting. "I got tired of the audition life. And I don't really think of myself as an actor."

"I don't think of myself that way either," Andy said. "What I think doesn't seem to matter."

Willem thought he might come back to that point later, when he had some time to consider it. "They threw you that part, didn't they?"

"They fucking did, and they threw me into it. I got so little direction we couldn't tell if they actually wanted me to tank." The memory was clearly annoying. "Thank God Victor knows what he's doing. Dana helped a lot. And once I was over the hump it was okay. But we wanted it to be good. We thought it was important. What it took was digging into some pretty deep shit, and oh yeah *that* sent me back to a shrink for a tune-up."

The idea of digging into his history for a part made Willem feel ill. "If that's what it takes, fuck it."

Richard put a hand on his thigh. "Our number in February was kind of rough for both of us."

Andy leaned back in his chair, studying them. "Look, art that's personal, if it's any good, almost always hurts. It took me a few years as a photographer before I risked something personal, and even then I might not have done it if I didn't have help." He stood up, went to the shelf over the counter, and pulled down a book. "Take a look at that. I have to get online for a minute."

The room was silent for about ten minutes while he did whatever he was doing and they looked at the book. It was an oversized but simple, black-canvas-bound hardcover with 'City of Angels 2007' written on the spine in silver marker. It clearly hadn't been made for the public. Inside was a credits page naming Dana Richardson as producer, Rory Atwood as model, Dmitri Vasko and Patrick Sarkisian as exhibit hosts. Then there was a section with twenty-four full-page images. Each had the location, date, time, settings, and other details printed on the facing page. Following that was a much longer section with what had to be every shot taken for the project, by location.

The pictures were all of Los Angeles at night, nearly all exteriors, either devoid of humans or with only Rory. Sometimes she was fully clothed, sometimes almost nude. Sometimes sharply in focus, sometimes blurred as if she'd moved during a long exposure. Sometimes there were streaks of light as if cars had passed. The lighting all seemed to be ambient, and always seemed to create a faint glow around Rory. She looked like a magical, or possibly imaginary, creature. The city itself was a dreamscape.

On the last three pages was an essay describing the show – hung at Shall We Dance – and a performance by Dmitri and his then-partner Irina, and the music they used. Then there was a note about playing Leonard Cohen's 'Tower of Song' before and after that performance. The lyrics were written in by hand.

Eventually Richard closed the book and looked up at Willem. They could both tell the whole project was about the cost of creativity. The isolation, the loneliness, and the never-ending search. "I want to hear that song now."

"It was Rory's suggestion." Andy might have been expecting this. He clicked something and the song began to play. When it ended, he said, "Based on the work you've done together so far, it's obvious you both have creativity and talent. If you ever want to work on a visual project that isn't a dance, let me know. I know other photographers, film people, whatever. Don't rule anything out, I guess. What I'm doing now is something I never expected to do. Don't think something has to happen at a certain time, or right away, or at all. Evolution doesn't happen overnight."

Willem gazed at him, thinking about what the older man had accomplished since giving up the stage. If he could do half as well himself, maybe this feeling of inadequacy would go away. He'd made a good start at the yoga career. He enjoyed coaching. And he had Richard, who said 'we will figure this out, we will be okay' with such conviction that Willem almost believed it. Richard, who loved him. "I'm going to talk to someone," he said, before he knew he meant to say it. "Maybe Dr. Simon will have an hour to spare. I don't want us to get too co-dependent."

"Helping each other deal with shit is partnership, not co-dependency," Andy said dryly. "But that reminds me, when are you getting married?"

Richard and Willem looked at each other and almost laughed, guessing where Andy heard about that. Richard said, "Next month. Rory's doing it for us."

"Good. Now I'm going to throw you out because I have six emails from our director and if I don't start answering them I will never have any peace." They all stood up and shook hands. Richard and Willem thanked Andy, then headed for the stairs. They didn't say anything to each other, only had a word with the security guard on their way through the back gate to Richard's car.

Before he turned onto the street, Richard said, "Where would you like me to take you? Your place, my place, or some other place? I don't need to be at Chrome till showtime. I don't really need to be there at all."

"I'd like to see it. See our student, see what else is happening. Do I look okay?" He'd changed from yoga gear into jeans and a sweater (crocheted by Karen) before brunch.

Richard loved the sweater. It was made of soft cotton and silk blend yarn in shades of greenish-blue. It would look great with his peacock jacket. "You look gorgeous. I want to change, though."

"Then let's go to your place."

"It'll be our place soon." They smiled at each other.

Chapter 21

Willem tried not to squirm in the should-be-comfortable club chair. Tried not to fidget, tried to make eye contact, and tried to breathe. He had to start, and he didn't know how, and he didn't want to. "I haven't been this nervous since my first tryout on Broadway," he said in a rush.

"Has Mr. Hollister told you a little about the process?"

"A little, yeah. He said it would be different for me, because I'm different."

Dr. Simon suppressed a smile. "I'm sure that didn't seem fantastically helpful. The main thing is, you're here to talk. You can say as much or as little as you want. The more you say, the more you'll get out of it."

"What about you? Don't you say stuff?"

"I will ask questions. I may have a comment here and there. A suggestion. But it's not my job to give you a solution to whatever is troubling you. It's my job to help you find your own solution."

"How is there a solution to being molested by my grandfather?" It sounded sharp, and abrupt, and wasn't at all what he meant to say. But having said it, he might as well continue. "He's dead. No one knew until he was dead. No one knew till *now*."

"Well, you're not going to get a law and order kind of solution, obviously." Dr. Simon made a note and then looked up, over the top of his reading glasses. "Why did you make an appointment with me?"

"Everybody in the damn world was telling me I needed to." A moment of silence. "And okay, I knew I needed to. I was this close to screwing up the best thing I've ever had."

"Were you? What made you think that?"

The next thing Willem knew, he was hearing a soft chime. He took a breath. Dr. Simon made another note, tossed his notepad over onto the desktop, set his pen down next to it, and said, "Well done today. I think you're ready for this."

"Did I just talk for forty minutes straight?"

"Yes, you did." A smile, almost affectionate, as if the therapist was proud of him. "How do you feel?"

It wasn't an idle question. Willem thought about it. Thought of one of his favorite movies, huffed out a laugh, and said, "I feel fine." He told Richard the same thing later, before changing the subject. "You like cats."

"Yes," Richard said, somewhat cautiously, as if he wasn't sure where this was going. "So do you."

"Exactly, and we can't have one in this apartment. So maybe in a year or so we could find a place where we can have one. What do you think?"

Richard smiled. "Maybe a place that would let us have a cat would let us paint the walls, too."

"And hang some drapery instead of these godforsaken vertical blinds." They were sitting close together on the couch, an Underground Cabaret DVD on-screen but forgotten. "Maybe a place with no carpet." He was grinning, because Richard was laughing. "I mean, this place is perfect because you're in it, but it would be so much more perfect with a little color."

"And a cat." Richard leaned over for a kiss. "I'll bet we can find a much more perfect place. You're so funny."

“Why, because I haven’t even officially moved in and I’m all, let’s not stay here?” Willem wrapped his arm around Richard’s neck, kissing that laughing mouth again. They were both counting the days to their wedding, and to Willem being officially moved in. They’d negotiated their new lease, Willem had pinpointed the least-annoying places to park, they’d run through the who-pays-what questions. It was all the next best thing to actual fun, because it meant every day waking up together, every night going to sleep together, being there for each other all the time. “I can’t decide how I want you tonight.” Richard leaned away and let himself fall back on the couch, sprawling attractively. Willem put a hand on his chest, started unbuttoning his shirt. “Apparently I want you like this.” His hand on skin now. Leaning close with his other arm on the back of the couch, caressing and exploring as if he didn’t know this skin to the millimeter. Richard hooked a leg over Willem’s knee. “Apparently you want me like this, too.”

He wasn’t doing anything else. Sometimes they both liked it this way. He would lie there and let Willem do anything, everything, as if they didn’t both know he was silently directing it all. Having this much power was almost scary sometimes. Richard savored the feel of that hand on his chest, rocking his hips almost by reflex when Willem’s mouth came down to his nipple. “Oh God, Willem.” Kissing, licking, sucking. “Oh *Jesus*.” The hand tracing the bottom of his ribcage, then down the middle to the button of his jeans. The zipper. Inside. Richard made a hungry sound, knowing that soon he’d be in Willem’s mouth. But apparently Willem wanted more skin.

He was using both hands to tug Richard’s jeans off, then his briefs. Hands and mouth on his legs, the sensitive skin on the inside of a knee, moving up his thigh. Lifting a leg and placing that foot on the top of the couch. "You should see yourself right now," he said. "I could make a million dollars with this picture." He wanted that cock so much he was salivating, but he looked up to see Richard's face. Dreamy, sleepy-eyed, a little flushed. "Tell me you want me."

"I want you."

"How do you want me."

"Every way." He arched his back as Willem swept both hands up his thighs, up his flanks, planting them beside his head as he went in for a kiss. Still fully clothed, his erection pressing against Richard's through fabric. "Oh God, Willem, in my mouth, please." He felt Willem's smile, muttered a frustrated protest when he moved away. Back down Richard's body, taking him in his mouth, making a happy sound as Richard surged under him.

"Mmm, you're close, aren't you baby." Teasing, only lips and a bit of tongue at the head. Richard whimpered. "God you taste good." Licking again, Richard's hand in his hair. "More? Like this?" A gasp, the other hand clenched on the cushion, thighs trembling. Willem took him all the way, expert at this man's pleasure, adding suction only when he reached the peak, hand flat to his groin with thumb and forefinger bracketing the base of his cock.

"Oh Jesus fucking God help me –" The next sounds weren't words. Willem backed off just enough to avoid scraping Richard with his teeth, otherwise holding position as he thrust up. Savoring the pulse, swallowing, absorbing the aftershock. His own cock was bound uncomfortably by his jeans. He eased his position, used one hand to undo the button and the zipper, sighed with relief. Richard felt it, because he was still in Willem's mouth. "Get that cock up here. Fuck my mouth." There was no argument. By the time Richard had the cushions adjusted Willem was kneeling over him, naked and rampant. Richard took him in hand and looked up. They were making eye contact before he closed his mouth, and then, Richard knew, Willem's head went back and his eyes drifted shut. He knew because he'd watched this before in the bedroom mirror. He knew if there was a million-dollar picture, it was this one. Willem's beautiful body, tense with the effort of restraint. Always careful not to hurt Richard, even when he was pumping into his mouth, swearing, gasping, coming. One of Richard's hands was on his hip, holding him off a little because once in a while, yes, there it was. Willem almost collapsing forward, the shift of weight before he caught himself.

"God *damn*." Catching his breath. Pulling back. "Okay?"

"I'm okay." Smiling as Willem sat down, half on top of Richard, as if all his strength had gone down Richard's throat. They both shifted, adjusting, getting comfortable.

"You're perfect."

"You are. I love you."

Willem stretched out with him, relaxing. "I love you too."

The May showcase was sold out. Their advance tickets got them a couple of barstools at the counter in the back of the downstairs lounge. "We would've had a better view if we were in the show," Richard said, amused by it all. He knew they'd be adding the production DVD to their collection. Even if they hadn't been days away from their wedding, and even if Karen wasn't their friend, they would have thought her number with Zach was one of the most beautiful, romantic things ever on the Chrome stage. They couldn't quite believe she and Zach weren't an item, and seriously doubted her allegation that such a thing hadn't even been discussed.

"Okay, it's one thing to see the Borodins do 'All I Ask of You.'" Willem was holding his forgotten bottle of Pellegrino, ranting a little. "They've been married for a while, they've been dancing together even longer than that, they're awesome, whatever. Then little miss yogi comes in here with her first number in fifteen years and I don't know about you but I was bawling."

"Oh, me too," Richard assured him, trying not to laugh. "That song gets me every time, but the way they hit the lyric was killer. They've never even kissed?"

"So she says." Willem took a swig of the sparkling water. "When they do, it's going to be fucking *epic*." They both cackled.

Richard located his glass again and had a drink. "We should do one of his songs sometime."

"Yes, we should." Willem leaned on the counter, angling in so their faces were close together. Remembering the days, so recently, when he would have stolen a kiss here because he wouldn't be able to later. He stole a kiss anyway. "What should it be? There are so many great ones. 'With One Look' would be fantastic."

"Or 'I Believe My Heart.' Not as many people know that one." Richard put a hand up to touch Willem's face, trailing his fingers down his neck to the bewitching hollow of his throat. "But I really think it should be 'Love Changes Everything.' Don't you?"

They were both smiling, but Willem was absolutely serious when he said, "Yes. I do."

Their wedding was everything they'd imagined. Finding a spot in the middle of the Urban Light exhibit, standing around as if they had landed there by chance. Karen, Sam and Mateo deployed to shield Willem, Richard, and Rory from incursions by other pedestrians. Dana oh-so-casually taking video with her phone while Rory performed the brief ceremony. Pictures with everybody's phones. Kisses, tears, laughter, and Willem doing his Gene Kelly impression on a lamppost until a security person started toward them.

They all walked up the street to Spare Tire. Richard conducted his rituals under cover of everyone else's general hilarity. It was strange to think that all these people knew exactly what his issues were. All of them let him be the expert. Cared enough about him to leave him alone and let him get on with it, washing down each bite with champagne.

Willem drank sparkling water, as usual. Sam drew the short straw for being the designated driver back to West Hollywood. Mateo, Dana, and Rory took full advantage of that. Karen artfully dodged questions about her and Zach, promising Richard she would finish his sweater now that 'Memory' was done.

Then, because it was a weeknight and they all had work the next day (except Rory, as she smugly pointed out), they asked for the check. Willem and Richard were not allowed to contribute. Dana cut off their protests with a distraction, saying, "I know you said no gifts but this didn't cost me anything, so hush." She pulled a small package out of her jacket pocket and handed it to Richard.

It was the unmistakable shape and size of a media disc. He glanced at Willem, who did a 'who knows' thing and tore open the wrapping paper. The disc case had a picture inserted in the front: 'The King and I,' Chicago 2000. Richard looked up at Dana. "Oh my God. Is this his?"

"Is it?!" Willem opened the case; there wasn't anything in there except the unlabeled disc itself. "How did you get that?"

"Well, Richard told me when you did it and I knew where you were. So I asked around. Six degrees of pesteration. Somebody knew the director, he knew the stage manager took video at dress rehearsal, and voilà."

"I get to hear you sing 'We Kiss in a Shadow.'" Richard couldn't believe it. "I get to see it. Dana, thank you." He was so blown away he couldn't remember, later, if he thanked and hugged everyone else.

Willem assured him he did. "You were perfect as usual. Do you want to watch that tonight, or save it for the weekend?"

"Of course I want to watch it tonight. But it's a long show, so let's save it for the weekend. We could do something else tonight." Richard set the disc down on the media cabinet and stepped into Willem's arms. They held each other for a long minute.

"I'm looking over your shoulder at my hand," Willem said softly. "Looking at this ring. I will never take this off."

"Neither will I." Each of them moved slightly, and then they were kissing.

Later, when they'd made it all the way past washing up to the bed, they lay facing each other. Naked, smiling, touching at hands and knees and feet. Willem said, "I had this idea that I'd want to fuck all night like a maniac after marrying you."

Richard laughed softly. "Me too. All I want to do is lie here and look at you and let my mind be blown because you're my husband."

"Right?" Willem leaned across the slight distance for a kiss. "But news flash, there will be fucking." He felt Richard's mouth curve against his, a smile that became a laugh and then a squeal as Willem moved in.

June 2018

Dr. Simon was at his desk when they went in. He stood up, came around, and shook both their hands. "Let's see those rings. Very nice. Have a seat, gentlemen." They chose the couch, so they could sit side by side. He arranged himself in his club chair, tapped his notepad with his pen, and said, "All right, Mr. and Mr. Hollister. Where would you like to begin?"

"Well," Richard said, with a sideways glance at his husband, "we're going to be in a movie."

Dr. Simon sat back, smiling. "Tell me more."

THE END

If you enjoyed TAKE EVERYTHING, please consider leaving a positive rating or review. It really helps! Thanks for reading.

Want more? MY HOLIDAY STAR also features characters dealing with mental-health issues. Rainbow Book Reviews says "This is how quality gay romance for grownups should be written."
Discover this world of romance at
www.thelastories.com

*****

About the Author

Alexandra Caluen lives in a small purple house with her husband, a bottle of Laphroaig, a lot of books, and nine pairs of ballroom shoes. She works in patent law and has enough hair for three people.

www.ingramcontent.com/pod-product-compliance
Lightning Source LLC
La Vergne TN
LVHW091129080826
845145LV00008B/2096

* 9 7 8 1 7 3 3 7 2 1 1 9 6 *